THE

DARK

OF

YOU

THE MISS HYDE COLLECTION III

KINDRA

SOWDER

THE DARK OF YOU Kindra Sowder

This Edition published by Kindra Sowder Media, an imprint of ELK Publications, in 2025 in the United States of America

ISBN: 978-1-967293-95-7

Copyright © Kindra Sowder 2025

Cover art by WJR Parks, 2025

Edited by Edd Sowder, 2025

Format by ELK Publications, 2025

The Dark Of You

The Miss Hyde Collection III

Kindra Sowder

THE DARK OF YOU   KINDRA SOWDER

CHAPTER ONE

All coherent thought left my mind, replaced with fear. Nevermind the rage beyond anything I had ever felt burning brightly just behind that fear. I wanted to scream. I wanted to shatter his beautiful face, but I settled for the glass vase on my penthouse's coffee table. Shards of glass, water, and red roses scampered across the marbled floor at my feet like frightened animals.

Jackson knew better than to follow me inside after leaving Adam's — Emmett's — apartment. When I left his office, I walked home, not even bothering to wait for the car. My feet ached badly, but didn't I deserve every ounce of pain I felt? Didn't I deserve the grief?

Reaching down, I gripped the edges of the glass coffee table and overturned it with a feral cry, shattering it quite effectively. My hands came up instinctively to protect my eyes, but I didn't really care if I hurt myself. I truly felt I would deserve it if it were to happen. What was a little more pain in my severely unsettled life?

Tears welled in my eyes, burning as they pushed their way out and down my cheeks. Glass crunched beneath me as I fell to my knees, then sat in the midst of my chaotic mess, nearly falling onto my rear — sobbing while the pieces of glass cut into my flesh under the long gown. My hands involuntarily balled into tightly clenched fists. I wanted to hit something. I wanted to cause damage. I wanted to cause harm. Emmett's — Adam's — face forced its way into my thoughts, only making the violent urges take an even firmer grip over my will. I slammed my fists into the floor, my skin stinging with the contact of dark oak, glass, and thorns against the hardened coolness of what was a perfectly unmarred floor. Blood seeped into the water on the floor like reaching tendrils.

His face never left, and my stomach churned. Slumping forward, the shards cut even deeper.

The revelation that Emmett was indeed Adam Burnside, a man dealt the same horrible cards as me, had come as a complete shock. So much so that all the painful memories that Hyde hid from me to save my

2

mind came flooding back with stunning — terrifying — clarity.

How it unfolded played in my mind repeatedly, drilling the information even deeper into my memory. Every piece of the puzzle fell further into place. Every part of my story purposely hidden from me came screaming back.

Closing my eyes, squeezing my lids shut to stop more tears from falling, I stood in his office yet again.

The shadows of the room fell over me, mask around my eyes. He wore no mask except that of Emmett's face. His eyes were bright blue, almost glowing in the dim light. Electricity zinged through my body as everything — every pain and every horror — flooded back.

"Emmett?" I whispered, shock taking over as my blood froze in my veins. "Wha—?"

The smirk on his beautiful face spread into a wide, knowing grin — turning him from a slightly comforting presence to a menacing one. Rising from the chair, he strode around to stand in front of me and sat on the edge of the desk.

"Not quite," he mused, stuffing both hands into suit pant pockets. *"Of course, neither of us is who we seem."*

My mouth fell open, uncertain of how to respond except to stammer.

"I… I…," I croaked.

"Are we, Blythe?" he asked, startling eyes meeting mine with incredulity.

"I... I… guess…" I stuttered.

My heart pounded, sweat broke out over my entire body, and adrenaline poured through my veins at the onslaught of horrid images that flashed through my mind. But not just that. My cells sang with the electric feeling of pure and abject terror.

I wanted to run. I wanted to run as fast as possible away from the uncertainty that blossomed in me. Most of all, I wanted to run so that I could finally fall to my weakened knees.

"What is it, Blythe? Are you…" he paused, an eyebrow raising in mock concern, *"afraid?"*

I fought the urge to nod. I couldn't show the fear I felt. Not even as the images of bloodied, open female

4

bodies entered my mind. Not even as the sights and smells from Johan and Mitch's assault — and ultimately, their deaths — barged in. The frog lodged in my throat was uncomfortable, but I swallowed it down, effectively clearing it away only to settle as a solid pit in my stomach.

"I'm not afraid," I said, voice coming out weak and miniscule. "Surprised is all." Louder this time.

He nodded, seeming to ponder that for a moment before removing a silver lighter and small case from his pocket, flipping it open to reveal hand-rolled cigarettes. The sight of them caught me even more off guard. Emmett had never once smelled or tasted of tobacco. He removed one, stuck it between his lips, put the case back in his pocket, and flicked the lighter open. A small flame erupted from within the metal canister.

"I see," he muttered around the cigarette, lighting it in the same breath.

Squaring my shoulders, I attempted to exude the pride I felt in myself. Tried to use the strength Hyde lent me to survive the coming moments, whether physically or emotionally violent — or both.

"I wanted to meet sooner, you see, but Emmett is a stubborn one. Wanted to have all your attention despite my… desires."

His eyes flicked up to me again as he drew on the cigarette, smoke pouring out from between his lips and his nostrils with the last word. My body trembled slightly as I stood there watching him. Even in Emmett's body, I knew what Adam was. I knew exactly without him having to introduce that part of himself at all.

My bravado finally kicked in, Hyde pushing slightly forward within me to give me the edge that was desperately needed. The heat in my eyes was unmistakable.

"You could have just taken the wheel," I said, tilting my head to the side.

I saw him notice the slight change with a glint in his eyes and a wicked smirk on his lips. Taking another draw from the cigarette perched there, he leaned against the desk again.

"Touché." Adam sighed. "But it seems I have underestimated his feelings for you. He has managed to take more control than I would like. See," he paused, taking another puff on the tobacco, "when he feels, it is

intensely. So much so I sometimes have trouble controlling him."

"And you're telling me this, why?"

"Because, Blythe, you are a very special case."

Confusion set in — for both Hyde and me. My brow furrowed, causing Adam to laugh, sultry and horrifying all at once. That was the allure of those like us, I suppose. We are good, and so bad all at once. We pulled on that human sense of duality most hide from and forced them to meet it head-on. After meeting us, they had no choice, and they were far beyond saving.

"Because he deeply cares for you, and you work symbiotically with your demons. We do not. We fight for control, especially where you are concerned."

The confusion must have been evident on my face because Adam sighed and drew on the hand-rolled cigarette again.

"We are both drawn to you — to you and your other half, Blythe. We both love you, and we both hate you. I believe, when it comes to love, Emmett feels it much stronger than I do, but I still feel it all the same. And it pulls at me when you are near because I don't only love you, Blythe. I love your monster as well."

7

THE DARK OF YOU   Kindra Sowder

My head shook involuntarily while Hyde writhed with lust and anger within me. I wasn't sure how much more I could take before losing myself and my mind completely. Yes, the words he just spoke were wonderful — what every woman wants to hear. But he had lied to me. Pretended to be someone he wasn't in a way. Emmett wasn't Emmett. Adam wasn't Adam. Both Emmett and his monster hid behind masks, and willingly left me in the dark. A darkness that was willingly able to consume me if I allowed it.

Adam walked toward me with arms outstretched. I hadn't even seen him put the cigarette out. The tendrils of smoke rose into the air, filling it with its pungent aroma. Stopping in front of me, his fingers grazed my lips, and I felt something awful stir inside of me. Hyde reacted, and not in the way I expected. She lusted after the man before me. So did I, but wrath and fear took over the instant his flesh touched mine.

"Don't," I felt myself growl, deep and low in my throat.

Heat flared in my eyes and in my belly, both mine and Hyde's presence stirring and swirling together to join forces.

8

Adam's blue eyes flashed as he grinned, seeing the monster he claimed to love. Then I saw something underneath the cockiness. A sadness seemed to move through him, tears twinkling along his lids, and jaw clenched. Emmett was definitely in there. The changes in Adam's cocky demeanor told me so much more than his beautiful words. How could I hate him? He was an unwilling passenger like I was, right?

I couldn't be so sure anymore.

"Please, Blythe," he breathed, moving his hand to cup my cheek tenderly, looking deep into my eyes as if he were speaking not only to me but the monster that resided there too. "Accept me."

That was when Hyde and I locked together. Those same words. Used over and over to win an ultimate battle. Words Hyde had used when speaking to me when I struggled with what we were.

Before I could stop myself, or Hyde, my hands pushed against him, and he let me do it. He slammed into the front of the desk, hands going out to stop a fall, but knocked various office items onto the floor instead. The lamp was the last to fall, shattering on the floor with a bright flash of light as the bulb broke.

9

THE DARK OF YOU   KINDRA SOWDER

"Don't you dare," we yelled, her voice mingling with mine.

I barely saw the hurt and unmistakable anger in his eyes before I turned, opened the door, and ran as fast as I could before ending up back at my apartment.

Now, I sat here, covered in glass, water, and my own blood in a beautiful dress that I was destroying. I found myself not caring.

Opening my eyes, I looked down at the gorgeous red gown that sheathed my body. The anger rose up in me again, bringing Hyde forward until we merged into something uncontrollable. The need to destroy rose up again, my hands coming up to grip the bottom hem of the dress that I could reach. The sound of ripping fabric was oddly satisfying, and I felt the sinister grin spread across my lips.

After a few moments — moments I barely remembered through Hyde's haze — shreds of fabric were all that was left of what had been something so beautiful. Something now destroyed. Another thing destroyed by my affliction. Score one more for the monster within.

THE DARK OF YOU Kindra Sowder

I slammed my fists into the pile, and let the rage and grief overtake me.

"Fuck," I screamed, animalistic and tortured as tears reemerged.

I screamed again, wordless. I didn't even care if I roused the neighbors. If… and it was a strong *if*… they could hear me through the floors I had specially made when I purchased this loft penthouse, they would probably ignore it either way. I imagined them thinking it was just that rich bitch upstairs throwing a tantrum. If only they knew the truth. If they did call the cops, I was fairly certain Detective Bell would come calling. He already seemed to suspect my involvement in missing men during our brief conversation.

Another headache I did not need.

You'd need that like a hole in the head, Hyde said inside my skull. *This Adam shit is enough.*

And just like that, the pure wrath I felt came rampaging back, Hyde rising along with it until we were one again. Every part of me burned with her, and I couldn't fight her. I'm not even certain I wanted to.

Her hunger was overwhelming, but I knew how she would indulge tonight — for my sake. Saving me from another trauma despite how horrific her intentions were. Standing up, dressed in only my matching bra, panties, and heels, my blood covered legs took us into the kitchen and straight to the freezer to what lay within.

The stainless-steel door flew open as soon as we touched it, almost breaking it off its hinges. The neat stack of butcher paper-covered organs greeted us like a close friend. A white cloud of chilly air passed over us as we greedily reached inside, almost running to the microwave to defrost them. I felt Hyde's urge to rip into the paper and into the frozen hearts, but she rethought it to spare the teeth we would always need. Our hunger was ravenous. I couldn't say, even to myself, that what was about to happen wasn't welcome. Our needs to terminate and to tear and to shed blood had become one, both of us taking part in the same macabre dance.

I hadn't even noticed my hands place the packages in the microwave and hit the defrost, or that every package in the freezer now lay at our feet, thawed with blood seeping out of the butcher wrap onto the floor.

I didn't care. There was only one important thing in the room. One thing that would keep Hyde from taking to the streets. The level of hatred and wrath could have been strong enough that I feared she'd take and kill more than one man that night. That would be more than enough for the detective to come sniffing around again. Of course, I was certain he hadn't stopped.

I felt the growl in our shared throat before I heard it, then felt the impact of our knees on the marbled tile floor. My skin slithered against the tiles slick with the barely warm blood, and our hands reached out, taking one package, and ripping it open — scarcely stopping to breathe before our teeth sank into the defrosted muscle. The taste of meat and iron filled my mouth, and I would have gagged if Hyde weren't halfway in control. I didn't dare stop her. She needed this. In a way, I needed it as well. The sensation of our joined urges was hard enough to understand, explaining it would have been much more difficult, so I didn't bother to think about it.

I rode the sensations, and let the meat roll around in my mouth one after another. Blood coated my hands and dripped down my arms and chin, down to my belly, and soaked into my lingerie. It was warm and cool all at once. Slick and sticky and congealed all at the same time.

It felt like Heaven. Pure unadulterated bliss. Finite bliss, but that was all right. There was an endless supply outside of the walls of the apartment.

Teeth ripped into each heart, paper ripped away and discarded on the floor. Blood coated everything. And it filled our body and soul with sex-like ecstasy. Heat, rage, and newly God-like power flowed through every vessel and into every cell, penetrating our deepest and darkest parts.

I no longer felt like a piece of me was shattering but strengthening with the power of a wildfire.

The last piece of male flesh slipped down my throat, my body oozing with sensuality and animalistic lust and rage. Every part of my inner core ignited, Emmett's face — eyes bright blue and the sensation of his inner demon stroking my skin — flashed through our collective mind. It only drove the sensations further, and our heart slammed in our chest, threatening to escape. My cells sang with electricity as I sat, shoulders slumping as we reveled in it with a heavy sigh.

THE DARK OF YOU Kindra Sowder

This was needed, and there was something else. A need for something more. I also felt her pull back, and for that I was thankful. My own mind was a tangled mess of what I had endured through Adam's actions no matter how indirect, and I couldn't stomach it.

Not anymore.

My stomach turned and nausea filled my mouth with saliva. So much that Hyde pulled all the way back, falling into the darkness, and let me take the reins while she hovered just within. The sensation felt deep within my chest was almost like the snap of a rubber band, and I knew she was relinquishing control.

Gagging, I shuffled away from the horrific mess and toward the bathroom, leaving a bloody trail the entire way. By the time I made it to the toilet, all control was lost with bile sour in my mouth. What I vomited was not anything I could, nor would ever want to, describe to anyone outside these four walls. Since nothing had time to digest before I wretched, chewed pieces of raw heart muscle floated below me along with congealed and partially broken-down blood. I gagged again and didn't stop until my stomach was completely empty of its contents. By then, the only thing to come up was stomach acid, which quickly turned into dry heaving. Even though everything I had ingested now had a new home, I could still taste the iron mixed with bile.

Sitting back, hair plastered to my forehead with copious amounts of sweat, a shiver ran down my spine. The marble was cool, almost welcoming, as I sat there with eyes closed — breathing deeply through my nose and out through my mouth with pursed lips. Slow and steady. Not too fast or I would be back in the same position over the full toilet bowl.

"Ugh," I groaned, placing one hand over my belly as if it would help. "Dammit."

That was the moment I realized nothing would. I felt all the unwelcome sensations of what had been done to me again. Kyle's near rape, but I didn't remember any of that after the drug he slipped in my drink took me. All I remembered was the loss of control right before everything went black. He worked for Adam, and instead of continuing his watch, he took it too far. Good for me. Not so good for him

Then the retaliation by more of Adam's men followed after I left his mutilated body on their doorstep. Somehow, Hyde had known, but *how*? How did she know where he came from and where to return him?

Nothing as far as that was concerned made sense.

Was the abduction, torture, and eventual rape *her* fault? How would I even know? Unless I asked.

My eyes snapped open, and I scrambled from my position on the floor, moving to the mirror where I knew I could maybe get answers. Hair still plastered to my forehead, face, and neck, and skin flushed, I glared at my reflection.

"How? How did you know?" I asked through ragged breaths.

The brown in my eyes flickered to green, then back to its normal brown as my skin tingled. As quickly as it was there, it was gone.

"How, God damn it? How did you know?" I growled and screamed, slamming my open palm into the mirror, cracking it into a webbed array of dishevelment.

A fractured shard sliced my hand open. I cried out in pain and blood flowed freely into the sink.

17

THE DARK OF YOU Kindra Sowder

"We had an agreement," I seethed, my hands gripping the edges of the sink. It stung, but I ignored it, glaring at myself as my skin crawled and my image splintered along with the glass. "You mother fucker. We made a fucking deal!"

My fractured reflection split off, some pieces filled with my angry expression, and others lips slowly curling into a knowing smile — eyes vibrant green.

"You're not ready," Hyde growled through my lips. "All in due time, you idiot. Clean yourself up. Then we can talk."

"Tell me," I cried, more tears starting to well in my eyes but not my reflection. She was in complete control of her emotions. "I need to know how you knew where he was. Please, Hyde. I'm practically begging. I'm at your mercy here."

My reflection shrugged with her coy smirk antagonizing me to a point of annoyance, but I knew she was playing with me. The worst part was I couldn't do a damned thing about it.

"Look you little whore, get that shit off you. Go to bed. We'll work together, so I'll give you what I've got, but you won't fucking like any of it. You'll have company tomorrow, so get your shit together and listen to the man. Trust me."

"Why can't you tell me now?" I asked, staring brazenly back at myself in the mirror's jagged reflections of my other self.

Hyde shook her head, menacing grin falling away.

"Trust me, Blythe, baby. You'd rather see it than hear it."

"This was your fucking fault. All of it. Just know that," I huffed before walking away from my reflection as Hyde sadly shook her head in her nonchalantly infuriating way.

I wanted to turn back to that mirror so badly and give her a well-deserved piece of my mind, but I walked to the shower instead. I turned it on and stepped in, panties and all, stripping them off as the scalding water touched my skin. I threw them into the far corner. They'd get a decent enough rinse.

As the water poured over me, every single thing that had been done to me since this affliction entered my life flashed before my eyes, only causing my anger and hatred to grow.

CHAPTER TWO

Sitting on my bed in a cotton nightgown, a glass of red wine in one hand and a sleeping pill in another, I stared off into the darkness of my bedroom. The alarm read four a.m., which made me groan. Luckily, I didn't have to be at the gallery the next day.

I glanced down at the pill, wondering if Hyde would truly divulge any information. When she said to go to sleep, was she hinting at providing the information through my dreams? One could only hope she wasn't being… well… Hyde. I knew better than anyone how much she liked to play games. Although, we have worked most of that bullshit out. Notwithstanding recent events coming to light, she still liked to play in the darkened recesses of my mind when she could.

There was only one way to find out, and I knew I wouldn't be able to fall asleep without the tiny pill's assistance regardless.

Tossing the bitter tablet in my mouth, I washed it down with the entire glass of wine. Probably not the best idea I had ever had, but it would do in a pinch.

Besides, it's not like the wine and meds would last very long in my system. Hyde would make certain of that. For both of us. In the darkness, I heard the door to my apartment open, then a soft curse belonging to Jackson followed.

"Blythe?" he called out.

I didn't bother answering. What was the point?

Footsteps came down the hallway and stopped at my bedroom door. The doorknob jiggled, drawing my gaze, but I didn't move. I just sat there staring at it. Maybe if I did long enough, he would go away. I softly set the glass down on the bedside table.

"Miss McAlister, are you all right?" he asked.

A sob choked me, but I swallowed it down along with the pain that I felt resurface. Instead of responding, I lay down on my side, bringing my folded hands to my chest, and let the medication and alcohol wash over me. It wasn't long before my eyes felt heavy, fluttering closed. I couldn't open them back up, and the world fell away as if it never existed.

The darkness that came over me was a welcome friend, taking all pain, grief, and regret with it.

THE DARK OF YOU Kindra Sowder

Until it wasn't the complete utter darkness anymore.

I was in a room with stark white tiled walls, covered in splashes of bright red blood. I felt warmth under the soles of my feet, sloshing over my toes. Looking down, the massacre on the floor almost made me gasp. My cotton gown was even covered in blood spatter, and there was no door to escape through.

Fear licked up my spine, causing my heart to race so hard I felt it beat within my throat.

Running up to a tiled wall, I slapped my palms against it and screamed.

"Let me the fuck out of here! Hyde!"

"Oh, for fuck's sake, Blythe. Can you *please* stop shouting?" my own voice came from behind me. "I honestly cannot hear myself fucking think."

I turned around, seeing a figure in the far corner covered in a sourceless darkness. The figure stepped forward, and all I saw was my own face, my own nude body with green eyes and covered in streaks of fresh blood.

THE DARK OF YOU Kindra Sowder

"I mean, God damn," the figure I knew to be Hyde halfway rolling her eyes at my weakness. "Has anyone ever told you you're fucking loud before?"

She reached up, placing the tip of her pinky finger in her ear, giving it a slight wiggle as if she were trying to regain her hearing after a concert. Turning toward her, I dropped my arms to my side and stopped fighting against the restraints of my own consciousness. This was her world. Always had been. And there was no escaping no matter how hard I tried. This place resided in the darkest corner of my own mind. *Her* territory.

Hyde dropped her hand at her side, not even bothering to cover her breasts, or anything else for that matter. She didn't care. Never had. When she took another step toward me, she stepped into a larger puddle of blood, and one single ruby drop trickled off one finger and down into it – splashing with one faint *drip*. A shiver moved up my spine, and she must have noticed it because she smirked and took another step through the pool of crimson.

"You asked for this, you know?" she said, eyes watching me carefully.

"I don't remember asking to be locked in a room with you," I responded, meeting her eyes.

She took a deep breath and continued her approach, shaking her head in disappointment.

"Maybe not, but you did ask for me to tell you how I knew, didn't you? This is how I can show you what I know, and how. If you don't want to know, all you have to do is wake... the fuck... up," she said sternly, "and don't bother asking again."

I stared at her for a long moment, and when she stopped directly in front of me, I released a heavy sigh. Maybe I did ask for it. Not for this specifically, but I did want to know how she knew about Emmett and Adam. How did she know where to drop Kyle's body after she slaughtered him? How did she know any of it? How could she not tell me any of it to begin with?

"I didn't tell you to protect you, Blythe," she answered.

"What the...? How...?"

She used her index finger and tapped against her right temple.

"How do you think? Don't be so goddamn naïve."

THE DARK OF YOU   Kindra Sowder

My eyebrows rose. I was highly irritated by her attitude, and slightly entertained. She had always been snarky, but I wasn't expecting her blatant disregard for my treatment at that moment. Not with what I knew was coming. Of course, I couldn't say I was making the exchange easy on her.

"Can you try not being a bitch first?" I asked, using the same tone she just had.

Her eyebrows rose as well, but with shock, her mouth almost falling open. Then she grinned and nodded, eyes turning intense as they met mine once more. The bright green of them was stunning – green irises framed by a dark ring of black and speckled with gold flecks that only made them brighter. A color I was stunned no man before ever really found weird, but we all know they weren't looking at our shared pair of eyes. They were looking at the perky breasts and slender form before them. Only the body that would pleasure them mattered.

"You block me out, Blythe. It's one reason you didn't realize Emmett wasn't exactly honest with you about who he was."

"That," I began, "and that you hid it from me."

"For your own good. You weren't ready for the truth. And quite honestly, you still aren't, but I have no choice now. Adam forced my hand."

I felt hysterical laughter bubble up my throat, and it wasn't long before it came spilling out onto the floor around us, creeping across our flesh. It was a mixture of the reality of what was happening and fear. Maybe she was right. Maybe I couldn't handle what she was about to tell me. But that didn't even matter. I would probably never be ready to hear it, but that didn't change the fact that I needed to know. Not just for Hyde, but for my own sanity. I was breaking at the seams after the revelation that Adam and Emmett shared the same body and mind. This wouldn't make it any better. If anything, it would bring everything back into focus.

"Wait, what? He... forced your hand?" I asked through my panic-stricken laughter. "Are you fucking kidding me? Do you realize how ridiculous that sounds?"

With a nod, she glanced away from me, and then back with a fervent stare that caused my laughter to catch in my throat, stopping abruptly. Her grin was gone, and her lips were set in a thin, aggravated line. She was clearly angry.

"We had a deal. Either you let me in and stop blocking me out, or the deal is done. I tried to keep you safe from this as best I could until you were actually ready to hear or see any of it. Do you realize what all I have kept from you to keep you sane?"

"This is sanity? This?" I spun around in a quick, tight circle coming back to face her again. "Huh?" I asked, throwing my hands up to gesture toward her. "Standing here in an imaginary place inside my head is obviously a true rendering of someone who is completely sane?"

"A lot saner than if I had let you remember every little thing, Blythe. Now you will, and I can't hold any of it back. This could break you. I need you to understand that."

I met her gaze, tears pricking at my eyes as the rage, grief, and sadness came flooding back. One escaped its prison and cascaded down my cheek, warm and filled with horrors.

"Like I'm not already."

My voice was low but eerily cold, even for her.

THE DARK OF YOU Kindra Sowder

Hyde froze, perfectly still in something akin to shock. She examined me with only her eyes, and her appraising stare caused me to crumble even more. More tears forced their way out and my chin trembled as my knees began to shake. The longer she stared me down, the more I broke inside. I wanted to know. I needed to know. How did she know these things? How did she know where Adam was in order to drop Kyle's body at his doorstep? There was only one way to find out.

As I watched, she seemed to make a decision and put her hands out toward me palm side up. Her hands were still, no visible signs of anxiety, nor fear. She didn't sway, she didn't breathe heavily. The terror was my affliction, and I was beginning to show every sign that I had been trying to hide it. I shouldn't have. She had seen it all in my outburst when I entered my apartment.

"I'll give you all I've got. I'll just need you to take my hands," she said, voice firm with a hint of comfort.

I brought my hands up, hovering just over hers with hesitation. They trembled visibly, and I took a deep breath in an effort to steady myself. It didn't work. All it did was bring a sob from my throat.

THE DARK OF YOU Kindra Sowder

"You just have to trust me," she continued.

I looked up then, meeting her bright green eyes. All I saw within them was honesty and pure, unadulterated will. That was all it took. I slammed my shaking hands into hers, and she gripped them so hard her nails dug deeply into my flesh – drawing blood. As it flowed down, dripping into what we stood in on the floor, my vision flooded with the same crimson. My head shot back, and the involuntary scream fled my lips as Hyde forced her way further into my mind.

Electricity forced its way into my skull, and then through my nerves to overtake my entire body. It hurt like Hell, and the next scream that left my lips was on purpose. As was the next to follow. I wanted to let go. I felt myself jerk against her, but I also felt her grip me even tighter with each pull.

"Don't you dare pull back now, Blythe," I heard Hyde say, but I couldn't see her.

The red had completely taken over, then images and voices pushed into my awareness. Then I was standing in the city, and my name was being screamed by a multitude of voices that I didn't recognize. My vision faded to black, and everything I knew she wanted me to see came in flashes of imagery. I smelled the musky dank of the city, and then I saw myself walk out of my apartment building, almost like I was watching through someone else's eyes. I felt the rapid heartbeat inside the body of the person, and then it was as if I separated from myself, and Emmett's – Adam's – face came into view. Eyes a stark blue.

He had been watching me. Always watching.

Then I was at the bar, Kyle pouring me a drink with a little something extra. I stumbled out of the building and passed out before waking up at his apartment. It wasn't covered in his blood... yet. He stood over me as I lay on his bed, the world still spinning with the drug, mouth moving as if he were speaking. I couldn't hear what he said. His voice slowly emerged from the silence.

"I know Adam wants you, but what kind of man would I be if I handed you off to him without having a taste first?" he said, rubbing his thumb over my lips.

I saw myself get up and take his throat in my hands. I questioned him, beat him until he told me who Adam was and that I would be disposing of him when I was done. That the message should be perfectly clear after he saw the gift I would leave him. He gave Hyde everything she needed. Emmett's address. The same apartment building I had visited when I learned the truth.

Then I was in the hallway of his apartment building, dropping Kyle's lifeless body on Adam's doorstep. The door flew open, and Emmett's lovely browns met my own, but I knew he didn't see me. He saw Hyde. His face twisted in horror, but then there was a flash of blue that told Hyde everything she needed to know. It wasn't like she was shocked by the revelation at all. She had known on some level before. My torture and rape ran through my mind next, and I relived every dreadful second up until Hyde slayed them for what they had done.

Every encounter with Emmett replayed after that, and there were small things Hyde noticed that I completely missed. The simple flash of color in his eyes – easily missed if you weren't paying attention. There were moments when his actions didn't look like Emmett was in the driver's seat – his own version of the same monster I kept inside rolled around inside him. I felt when Hyde took notice of him. I felt the heated sensations and the danger lurking just underneath. I felt it all.

Most of all, I felt the darkness within him.

THE DARK OF YOU KINDRA SOWDER

My heart broke and I shattered, the sensation of Hyde leaving my mind zapping me back into focus. The black and crimson fled to an unknown home, and my knees buckled as soon as the white walls came into view. My kneecaps hit hard, sending a shock of pain through my legs and lower back, but Hyde didn't let go. Her arms came around me and the sobs came flooding out of me as if a dam had been broken.

What was I supposed to do with all this? I broke, but there was something deeper that I felt in my gut I was supposed to do. But the grief gave no reprieve to think about. It hit in wave after wave of white-hot rage and agony.

How could he hide *this* from me? Especially knowing I had the same affliction.

"You sensed him all along?" I asked, dropping my hands and looking up into bright emerald.

Her face fell, and she moved her hands to my shoulders.

"I did but does that change anything?" she asked.

I shook my head, knowing full well that it didn't change a damn thing. I was angry. I was tired of the fight. I was fucking pissed. Rage wasn't even the word for the menagerie of emotions that boiled through my veins. I had fallen for Emmett, which was the most horrid thing about the entire situation. And the whole time...

This affliction... condition... *curse*... had taken so much from me already.

"So, what are *you* going to do about it?" Hyde asked, interrupting my thoughts.

"You mean, what are *we* going to do about it?"

CHAPTER THREE

The darkness of slumber lifted, grogginess taking its place – no doubt a lovely side-effect of the mixture of sleeping medication and wine chaser I indulged in the night before. My entire body ached, stiff from barely moving all night. I awoke in much the same position I fell asleep in, my head turned down slightly and legs pulled up so my thighs rested against my belly. The comforter rested lightly on top of me, trapping far too much heat. Turning over onto my back, a groan escaped my lips as each muscle stretched, and I kicked the blanket off toward the bottom of the mattress.

All the images Hyde showed me played in my mind over and over, but I was no longer filled with irrational rage. Instead, I was filled with sadness, hopelessness, and anger at the secrets and the lies. There had to have been a good reason Emmett kept it all from me. That much I knew. But what were those reasons, and what exactly could I do about it? More importantly, what *would* I do about it? Hyde asked me that before everything went dark again, but my heart hurt too much to even consider revenge of any kind at the moment. If revenge was even an option.

I needed time to process. Hell, I just needed time to figure out what to do next. Not about the situation itself, but in the next few minutes.

I placed my hands on the mattress to push myself off the bed — my hand stinging to the point a hiss left my lips. Jerking my hand up, I looked at my palms. Both were a mangled mess. From my history, I knew they were much better than they had been. I had slipped my hands into so much glass and so much blood had crept onto the floor that the faint cuts still raw were all that remained. I took a moment and counted the blessings that Hyde *did* give me. I would just have to be careful for another couple of hours, and they would be healed completely.

A loud noise snapped me out of my thoughts, my heart skipping a beat along with the sound. Something heavy had fallen in the apartment. A curse followed, the source a voice I recognized instantly. Just the night before he shared his story with me, something I appreciated more than he would ever understand.

Jackson.

THE DARK OF YOU   KINDRA SOWDER

That was when I noticed the scent of freshly brewed coffee in the air, and my stomach growled.

"Thank God, there's coffee," I sighed, heavy with relief.

Swinging my legs over the bed, my toes touched the cool floor, sending a chill up my spine. It didn't take me long before I crossed the threshold and made my way into the living room. Shock took over as I laid eyes on the rest of my apartment for the first time.

"What the…?"

Everything was clean. Immaculate. Like someone had spent the entire night cleaning up the water, glass, red roses, and splotches of my blood off the floor. Any sign of what had taken place here was long gone like it had never transpired. The only sign anything was wrong was the missing coffee table.

"Good morning, Miss McAlister. How did you sleep?" Jackson asked, startling me out of my stupor.

His massive form took up the entrance to the kitchen. He stood there, drying the glass plate from the microwave with one of my white kitchen towels.

"Ummm, yeah… yes. I slept okay. Thanks," I stammered.

"Do you want some breakfast?" he asked. "Or some coffee?"

I looked at him, stunned that he didn't bring up what he walked into the night before. Such a disturbing mess I wasn't exactly surprised he hung around until the morning. Nothing was as it seemed. The mess with Emmett and Adam, and now this surprise from Jackson, it was abundantly clear. Cyra's most recent change in behavior didn't help the sinking feeling in my gut either.

Every single thing in my life, even as far back into the past as before my affliction started, made no sense at all.

Then I really took a moment and thought about Jackson's question. My stomach turned at the thought of anything going into it that was either meat or meat adjacent. Which meant nothing would sit well that morning except for strong, black coffee. That was perfectly fine. I liked it black most days, anyway. I felt a kinship with the darkness and bitterness of it.

"Breakfast? No, thanks. I appreciate the offer," I answered as I moved to sit down at a barstool across from him.

I looked around the apartment, then peaked at the kitchen floor as he continued to polish the large piece of thick glass. He watched me carefully, a knowing look in his deep brown eyes. I hadn't realized before how worn and tired he looked, as if working for Emmett sucked the life out of him. I couldn't say that would surprise me. It did the same to me. I just had better and more expensive means to cover up my exhaustion. Now that I knew about Adam, though, Jackson seemed to notice something in me that he had never seen before.

"What?" I asked, looking at him and meeting his worried expression.

"Do you want to talk about it?" he asked, turning to place the glass back inside the microwave.

When he turned back toward me, his brow knit together, and he frowned. He was concerned, which I understood. I would have been too if I walked into the bloody mess he found. Then, when he came to my door to check on me, I didn't bother to answer. Did he blame me? I wouldn't have blamed anyone in my situation. Of course, he knew about it the entire time, so I wondered if I should have been angry with him as well. As I watched him watching me, his face moving through a wide range of emotions, I decided I couldn't be mad at him. He had shared so much of himself with me the night before. Maybe he had done so in hopes I would see Emmett's — Adam's — giving side. And not just the side that left a bloody path through the streets.

The problem was, either side wasn't really the problem. It was the mountain of lies he left on top of the bodies.

Jackson set down a cup of coffee in front of me. I hadn't even noticed him pour it into the white porcelain mug since I had been so deep in thought after his question.

"Talk about what?" I asked as I picked it up and blew on the steaming liquid.

His face changed from an understanding expression to that of exasperation as he reached for his own cup of coffee. When he looked at me again, his eyes were soft and caring, no hint of the irritation I had seen flash across his features. I took a sip and watched him for a moment, taking in the concern penetrating his deep-set eyes as the light in my kitchen bounced off his perfectly smooth scalp.

"You know he'll be coming today. He'll want to talk," Jackson said.

"Who?" I asked, setting my mug down on the counter and meeting his eyes for the first time that morning.

My attitude was extremely petty and childish. I knew that. But I felt I deserved a touch of pettiness after everything that happened the night before. Also, it was a pretty legitimate question, if I had to be completely honest. Which of the two that inhabited his God-like body would want to talk to me? Emmett or Adam? How was I supposed to know? His face flashed in my mind, nearly glowing blue eyes reminding me so much of my green ones when Hyde took over.

"Blythe," he said with a slight tilt of his head. "He's in love with you. You don't think you need to hear him out?"

I sat there for a moment, mulling his words over. Of course, he was right. I should hear Emmett out to see why he felt this was a secret he needed to keep. We were the same, both sick beyond most people's imaginings, but did that justify it? I lied to those I loved on a daily basis, so I wasn't exactly the right person to throw stones, was I?

As I sat there wondering about the double standard I placed Emmett in, Jackson refreshed his cup of coffee, watching me carefully as if I were a bomb about to go off. Hyde slithered within me for a moment, tendrils of her consciousness carefully caressing my own. While she was angry as well, she had already known about him. She had felt it since the first time we met. Even Jackson knew and didn't bother to warn me, but I couldn't be enraged with everyone I knew who kept it from me. I would be a hypocrite.

They had me. Damn it. They had me.

Jackson bent down and picked something up behind the counter. The box full of documents, and the worn journal, came into view — landing with a pathetic thud on the countertop right in front of me. I knew what was in that book. I had read portions regarding my own ancestor, but I was certain Jackson was about to tell me something about it all that I didn't know. Him and Cyra had dropped it off at my apartment, after all. They had to be aware of everything on every single piece of paper.

"Have you read any of this?" he asked me, raising his eyebrows.

I nodded.

"A little bit."

I took another sip of coffee.

"Read more. There's an entire section in that journal," he stated, pointing at the old book, "that you'll be extremely interested in. I'll even keep Emmett from coming by for a few more hours to give you a chance to sit down with it. You need to know *everything*."

I placed my coffee cup down on the counter with an angry huff.

"He lied to me. Do you really think I should talk to him? Really? Because there's a massive part of me that doesn't think so."

He looked me directly in the eye. Then rested his elbows on the counter next to the box, taking my small hands in his massive ones in a fatherly gesture. Something I hadn't experienced in years.

"You haven't kept your secrets, Blythe?" he asked.

"If I had known he was like me, I'm sure I wouldn't have, Jackson," I replied, using his name just like he had mine.

"Just take an hour, at least. Read the section on Adam in that book you stubborn, stubborn girl," Jackson said in the most loving tone possible.

It was clear he had grown to care about me during our brief time together, and I had to admit it was nice to have that kind of love in my corner without strings attached. It was almost as if my father was alive again as I looked back into Jackson's eyes. It was at that moment I gave in to him, a small grin spreading across my lips in a silent show of cooperation.

"God, you're just as tenacious as he is," Jackson lamented with a sigh, letting go of my hands and turning to leave the kitchen. He walked past the partition to the kitchen with his coat in hand, pulling his arms through it. "I'll get to his place and hold him off as long as I can so you can get a shower before he comes too. Most importantly, read that." He pointed to the book. "You'll know which section is his. It'll tell you a lot. I promise. Maybe then you won't be so hard on him."

THE DARK OF YOU   Kindra Sowder

All I could do was watch him as he went to leave, a small smile on his lips as he replaced his jacket and picked his wallet and phone up from the arm of the couch. Jackson reached the door in a few short strides, his dress shoes shining in the sunlight filtering in from outside. His fingertips touched the doorknob, but then he stopped and turned to me, eyes earnest.

"Blythe, Emmett is an amazing man. Don't forget that. And he's so in love with you I don't think he could continue without you. Just remember that," he said, eyes meeting mine.

What I saw in his eyes caused me to freeze with my refreshed coffee cup to my lips, steam condensing on my upper lip and tickling my nose. Hyde stirred inside me, feeling the same thing I did in that instant. Understanding moved through us both, causing my heart to lurch in my chest when Emmett's face forced its way into my mind — then bright blue eyes pushed forward, tainting it. Hyde's anger was now replaced by another feeling I felt was completely unwelcome when those blue eyes surfaced.

Without moving the mug, I said, "I'll try," and I meant it.

CHAPTER FOUR

An hour or so later, I sat on my bedroom floor surrounded by documents that just seemed to bleed together. With legs crossed and a glass of red wine in my hand that it was way too early for I held the massive book in my lap, easily finding the pages Jackson had referred to before he left.

Just like with my ancestor, there was a hand-drawn picture of Emmett — one eye brown, the other bright blue. I stared at it and hadn't been able to move past that page since opening it. The words beyond it could change so much in the grand scheme of things when it came to our relationship, but I couldn't make myself turn the page to read them. Did I want to delve into this by myself, or did I want to hear it straight from him? Technically, considering the handwriting littering the pages was his, I would be hearing it all from him. But a large part of me wanted to hear it come directly from his mouth. I wanted to hear the entire story in his voice, not my own internal monologue as I read his ink-laden words. It was bad enough that his serial killer alter ego gave me the news to begin with.

THE DARK OF YOU Kindra Sowder

My stomach turned at the thought of the monster's touch when he attempted to caress my cheek.

Had I overreacted when I slapped him and took off? I felt the familiar sting of the action in my palm, my nerves conjuring the sensation as a reminder.

I dropped my head into my hands, my mind racing as I thought about the previous night's events over and over. Hyde remained silent, letting me work through it all on my own. She had already helped a lot by giving me more information than I had been armed with before. Granted, I hated everyone felt like they needed to hide important things from me, but I couldn't blame them either. I had been pretty fragile after everything that happened leading up to this moment. It wouldn't have taken much for me to snap. I had held it together pretty well, considering.

The sound of my door opening and closing made its way down the hallway, followed by heavy footsteps. I recognized them instantly and took a long draw off the wine. Emmett had come just like Jackson said he would. I just hoped his eyes would be brown instead of blue. If a pair of bright blue eyes crossed the threshold, I wasn't exactly sure how I would react.

THE DARK OF YOU Kindra Sowder

My heart pounded, threatening to come out of my mouth, as those footfalls came down the hallway and approached my open bedroom door. Every muscle in my body was on fire, every nerve fiber vibrating with tension and anxiety. I placed the glass down on the floor next to me as my hands began to tremble. It felt like an eternity had passed before his boots finally appeared in the doorway. When I looked up at his face, deep brown eyes filled with despair greeted me.

My heart dropped into my stomach as relief rushed through me, causing my body to break out in a cold sweat. My entire body sagged as I sat there, and he noticed my reaction. A hurt look crossed over his face, and he nearly crumbled standing there in the doorway, his knees noticeably weakening as tears welled up in his gorgeous eyes.

"I won't hurt you," he said as he took a hesitant step forward and reached a hand out toward me.

I remained sitting and didn't move. I knew Emmett wouldn't hurt me. That had never been a part of the equation. It was the lies and the secrets that had been the problem. Knowing we were the same, he allowed me to believe I was alone, and that stung more than anything else.

"I know," I whispered, my eyes never leaving his face.

He noticed the book, completely crossed the threshold, and took a few more steps closer to me. Then he saw the page I left open and froze, eyes wide.

"So, you know everything?" he asked.

"No," I replied, closing the book and sitting it on the floor. I stood, closing most of the distance between us until there was a mere foot between our bodies. "I want to hear everything from you. Not some book. From you."

I emphasized the last two words by touching the center of his chest with my index finger, right over his heart.

He closed his eyes as if the small touch had soothed something in him, a tear escaping down his cheek. Even though he seemed relieved, he also seemed hesitant, and I felt it coming off him like the cigarette smoke from Adam's hand-rolled the night before. We stood there for a moment in silence, and when he finally opened his eyes again, they flashed bright blue. I placed my hand on his cheek and made certain our eyes met, the love I felt for Emmett pushing me further into learning and embracing his entirety. Adam included. The secrecy and my anger toward it began to fade as I stood there quietly with him, and Adam's intrusion almost pulled me back into myself and away from him. I hung onto him and allowed myself to feel only him.

"Just me and you, Emmett. It's just us. You can tell me," I whispered to him as I leaned closer. "Adam is not a part of this moment. It's just us."

I watched him as he seemed to force Adam back, making certain he could no longer intrude on our time. He swallowed hard and leaned forward until our foreheads touched. It was that moment I felt my own inner demon pull herself back into the darkness, letting us have the moment I promised.

"Just us," I heard him whisper, his minty breath warm and comforting on my face.

I didn't respond. I knew he was saying it more to himself — and to Adam — than anyone. He had to believe it would just be us. That no one else would be a part of this revealing moment. He was about to give me his story. Something deeply personal that his monster already knew and was intimate with. And he knew that if we were going to continue, I needed it all. Not just what Adam may want to share, but what Emmett knew

51

was necessary. I needed it in only a way Emmett could give me. Complete honesty built on the love we forged in such a short amount of time. Every part of us had bonded, monsters included. Both Hyde and Adam had confirmed that in a way.

He stood and took a deep breath, looking down at me with complete and perfect trust.

"Okay," he breathed, "I'm ready. I want you to know."

"Okay," I replied, letting the rest of what I could have said remain silent.

He took my hands in his and took a deep breath, closing his eyes again as if remembering. I watched his perfect face as sadness and pain moved across his features, making me wish he didn't have to bother with telling me anything. But it was necessary. If it weren't, we wouldn't have been standing there terrified of each other and what would happen next. Adam had made it necessary.

"I was born in Sparta, Greece. Back in the times before the Peloponnesian War. In those days, I was a Spartan soldier. In the prime of my life with a new wife and rising through the ranks. Nothing could stand in

52

my way. They came to me to take part in a ceremony that would bring a more formidable strength. I wouldn't be the only one there. A few friends of mine that I cared for were as well." He stopped, taking a shaking breath that I felt through his body. "Through the ceremony, they revealed this glowing rock. I blacked out as the ceremony went on, and woke up at home, but something had changed inside me. I could feel it before I even knew what it was. I was okay at first, but then I saw my wife for the first time afterward and I felt it taking over. I wasn't me anymore. It was like another presence had made its home inside me, and I couldn't stop it from making itself known to her."

Taking both of my hands, he brought them to his chest and held them over his heart. His heart beat erratically against my hands and blazing heat radiated from him, the familiar sweat caused by adrenaline damp under my palms. As I watched his face, pure grief made its way forward, pulling tears from his eyes and down his cheeks. I didn't move. I let him grieve because, in a way, I knew what was coming and I knew he was still in the grips of that grief after all this time.

"We made love that night, and then…" he drifted off, taking an even deeper breath in as he steadied himself for what came next. "Adam killed her. He ripped out her heart and left her corpse there for me to find. Ever since, I've just been carving my path through history. Haven't really drawn a ton of attention to myself." He opened his eyes, and a fire burned in them as he looked at me. "Until now. When I found you, I had to know you. I had to be with you. I had never felt such a pull to someone since my wife. You changed everything in me and… in Adam. I can feel it. I didn't want him to make it known like this. I felt we needed more time, but he insisted. And sometimes I don't have control over him. I'm so sorry."

"Shhhhhh," I sighed, curling my hands into his. "It's okay."

He shook his head, and more tears flowed down his cheeks. I took my hands from his and placed them on his face, using my thumbs to wipe those tears away. I didn't want him to be sad anymore. I didn't want him to be scared. I didn't want him to feel the horror he felt at who he was. I wanted to make it right again but didn't know how. His story was horrifying, and I was horrified for him. I couldn't explain the revulsion I felt toward his monster, but the monster came with

Emmett. And accepting him came with a certain level of acceptance of that monster.

We stood there in perfect silence for a few moments looking into each other's eyes, longing building between us. Every part of my body hummed with a need for him so deep it was absolute. The same need emanated from him. He placed his hands on top of mine, his palms so warm it was overwhelming. The heat moved down into my very core, causing Hyde to stir very little. She backed off quickly, letting us devote the moments here to just me and him. Neither of our monsters seemed willing to take it from us, no matter what happened next. It was a relief. I hadn't been without Hyde in years, and I needed these private moments so badly.

Emmett kissed my forehead, lips wet with tears and placed his forehead against mine once more. He took a deep, shaking breath that vibrated through his chest. He pulled back then, a fire alight in his lovely eyes as he opened his mouth to speak.

"I love you, Blythe. And it's not because of what we are. That has nothing to do with any of it. I love who you are without your monster. I love every part of you. Have since I first laid eyes on you," he said. "You have kept me from ending all of this, if that's at all possible. I've felt like my life can have meaning again away from the bloodshed. While Adam is very much a part of who I am, he could never take that away from me. Ever. I am so completely enthralled by you, so absolutely and entirely taken by you that I could never leave. I need you in more ways than you could ever know."

My eyes burned with tears as I watched his face as he spoke, eyes wide trying to hold them back. Those words were ones I had longed to hear despite Adam's presence inside him. I knew the love came from them both, but I also knew the words were all Emmett's. I felt that deep down and believed every single one of them.

"If you hate me, I completely understand, and I'll leave you alone. I'll give you all the time and space you need," he said as he removed my hands from his face with a poorly disguised sniffle and stood. He began to back away, hands trailing down my arms, showing his unwillingness to let me go. "I just wanted you to know everything, and now it's all in the open. The ball, as they say, is in your court."

He let go of my hand and turned away, making his way to the door to leave. My heart ached and the tears I had been holding back fell as my heart broke. He thought I hated him when that had been far from the truth. I loved him more than anything. More than myself. I had been angry and full of rage, but nothing close to hate for him ever surfaced.

"Emmett," I cried, agony building in me at the thought of him leaving.

He turned toward me, eyes red from crying. His face flushed as if he believed I'd let him walk through that door. His heart was breaking the closer he got to the threshold just like mine had been.

My head started to shake of its own will.

"I don't hate you. I could never hate you. Please," I sobbed, "don't leave me."

Those words were all it took before a wall broke inside me and all the pain I had been feeling and held back during our encounter came out in a rush. I saw the same thing happen when his body reacted to my words, the urge to jump to action evident in how his muscles tensed. Relief moved through his eyes, and his feet carried him back to me so quickly he practically ran to close the distance between us.

He wrapped his arms around me and pulled me into him, embracing me so tightly. My entire body reacted to his touch, fire lighting up in the center of my chest and spreading — each nerve ignited. A lick of fear made my heart skip a beat, but then I realized what I felt at that moment wasn't the same as when Hyde took over. This was me. It was my own reaction. It was one hundred percent me. It was that moment I realized that my love for him was much stronger than I thought before. The totality of it hit me like a ton of bricks in the center of my chest, taking my breath away.

"I love you," I breathed, taking in his scent as each breath came ragged.

He kissed me, long, deep, and desperate, my entire body igniting with that same fire over and over again until it overtook me. Chills erupted all over my body and sweat beaded along my skin. Our bodies pressed firmly together, feeding the hunger between us. My hands gripped his shirt, and he lifted me into his arms. My legs wrapped around him without a single thought.

"Make love to me," I whispered as I pulled back less than an inch from his waiting lips.

A growl started deep in his chest before my lips came over his again, and he walked us over to my waiting bed. He lowered me down gently, kneeling before me like a King would bow only before his Queen. His hands glided up my legs and up to my hips, hand gingerly moving underneath my shirt to my lower back in worship. I ran my hands through his hair, moving down until I traced his perfect jaw with my fingers. He turned his head and took one of my hands in his, laying gentle kisses on my palm as he closed his eyes. He began to trail kisses down toward my wrist, and then down my arm to my elbow. Taking my arm from him, I reached up with both hands and removed my shirt, revealing myself to him in a way that felt brand new.

I felt completely open to him unlike any time before, and I knew exactly why. All truth had been laid bare, and sunlight had made it into the shadows of our relationship. Everything, even this moment, was illuminated.

Even my own fear, which I could tell Emmett noticed as he reached his hands out to touch me again. Of course, I saw the same fear in him as his hands shook slightly. I was certain we shared the fear that our monsters would surface and rob us of this, but as I felt around in my mind, there was no detectable trace of Hyde to speak of. His eyes looked off to the side for a moment as soon as his fingers met the flesh of my bare thighs, and then he smiled and looked at me with no trace of that fear present.

"It's just us," he said with a soft, joyful laugh.

His eyes lit up at the prospect.

I nodded and didn't bother waiting anymore. I pulled his shirt over his head, and he let me, taking full advantage of the moments we finally had to ourselves. Something we both probably hadn't had in years. For him, more than likely centuries. I slowly lowered myself to the bed until my back met the soft comforter, and he followed me, rising from the floor to cover me with his body. The fire blazed in his eyes again as he hovered over me, raining soft caresses over my body.

Reaching down, I made quick work of the belt and his jeans while he managed to kick off his boots. His jeans opened to reveal perfectly chiseled abductor muscles. I unzipped him and shoved the pants down with his assistance. We were both hungry for one another, but after he threw them to the floor, the fire inside him was still present. It had commingled with a quiet anguish and longing that let me know this particular encounter wouldn't be like so many of the others we had had.

THE DARK OF YOU   KINDRA SOWDER

He lowered himself on top of me and kissed me again, soft and deliberate, before entering me. Every move he made was slow and unhurried — every kiss, every touch, every stroke.

We handed ourselves over to each other more than once that night.

CHAPTER FIVE

My mind had gone dark as sleep pulled me under. Then images flashed into my mind — turning into a sequence of events I would have preferred to forget. I knew my hands were responsible for anything taking place, and every sensation was amplified like being trapped behind Hyde had put them in stereo.

Darkness surrounded us, and we weren't alone. Emmett's form came from within the shadows, eyes glowing blue, hinting at Adam's complete takeover. He was completely nude, and I felt Hyde's reaction deep in my gut as heat moved through our entire shared body. Lust pulsed through Hyde, and every nerve ending within us fired strongly to life. I felt a chill move up our spine as he neared, the fine hairs on our arms standing on end. Our breath hitched in our shared throat, and it almost felt like all the air had been released from the room. And she didn't see anything else.

Only him.

He stood before us now, slinking in like a wild animal. His blue eyes were stunning, penetrating our green ones with deep desire. We were both on fire, but

THE DARK OF YOU   Kindra Sowder

I didn't want to be. I wanted no part of what I was experiencing. That didn't seem to matter as it continued. I couldn't close my eyes. I wasn't in control.

Hyde growled and writhed in front of Adam, reveling in the malevolence of his body and the monster inside it. I felt her need. I felt everything, even the pulsing between our shared legs that refused to carry me away even though that was what I wanted.

But then I felt it. A new warmth spread through us, and my mind began to bend to Hyde's will as if Adam's mere presence meant we both must bow to the desire that took over.

His large hand came up, his palm covering our breastbone. His skin meeting our bare flesh sent a thrill through us, causing our shared heart to skip a beat. Our breathing picked up its pace as he pushed slightly, both of us giving in and taking a few steps back. Our back hit something cold, and when Hyde looked back, she spied something I had only seen in certain circles. Not ones I ever took part in, but Lauren had on plenty of occasions.

A St. Andrew's Cross stood upright behind us —
the cuffs attached gleaming in the one light in the room. At that moment, she saw beyond the shadows.

THE DARK OF YOU KINDRA SOWDER

The room was larger than our kill room, and the walls were lined with a much grander array of things to inflict pain, suffering, and death. She noticed the iron smell of blood infiltrated her nostrils, and she took a deep breath in.

That only compounded her lust, adding a bloodlust into the mix that I couldn't stop. Everything within her — and me — reacted to every sight, sound, and smell.

A seditious grin spread over Adam's lips, twisting Emmett's beautiful face into something unmistakenly nightmarish.

"I've been waiting for you," Hyde purred as she raised our arms above our head, a willing participant in his sexual games.

Adam laughed using Emmett's voice, and I heard the power within. It rocked me to my core but only spurred Hyde on.

"Here I am," he said as he leaned forward to whisper in our ear.

He reached up and placed Hyde's wrists in the cuffs, cinching them down as far as they would go so they bit into our flesh. She moaned as the metal pinched into it, jerking on the cuffs so it pinched harder.

Adam bit his lower lip, his need obvious in the set of his face. The need for pain and suffering, no matter how small. And Hyde felt the same.

This takeover was not welcome. I didn't want to feel or see these things.

Then, over his shoulder, a pulsing green glow made itself present as if both Hyde and Adam being there brought it to life. He spied how Hyde's eyes drifted in that direction and grinned. Turning toward it, his body drifted lithely in its direction.

What our joint eyes saw left me astounded, and recognition hit despite never having seen it before. Not really, anyway.

A statue of a woman, dating much farther back than his Spartan origins, came into view. A bright, green stone glowed, illuminating the space. Dark gray rock covered some of it, showing the shape of a voluptuous, primal woman. Placing his hand on it, he turned back to us and smiled. The light grew brighter at his contact, recognizing him.

THE DARK OF YOU Kindra Sowder

"This is what made us. She makes us strong," he explained. "She brought us to life, and with her, we will continue to thrive."

Seemingly out of nowhere, a broad knife appeared in his hand, glinting in the green light. The sight of it made our shared heart hammer even harder with knowledge of what may come next. His gaze never left us as he dragged it across his large palm, not once groaning with pain, and placed his bloodied hand on the belly of the statue. Deep crimson blood flowed from underneath his palm, flowing down pulsating green and gray stone like a thick river. The glow from within the statue gave way to a thrum that sounded like a million racing hearts. Ours beat even faster at the thought of the feast that it promised.

Adam turned to us, smiling with delicious wickedness, each muscle in his face standing out with glaring clarity. It could have just been the light, but it twisted his face into the maniacal monster we knew lay within. One that would lay waste to any that crossed its path. Did it require a harsh word, or violent action as the trigger? No.

All it required was the promise of flesh and blood.

THE DARK OF YOU KINDRA SOWDER

He stalked toward us, like a hunter approaching its prey. Neither I nor Hyde feared him. I knew he wouldn't hurt me because then that would prompt retaliation from Emmett in more ways than one. Dealing with my monster, who continued to track Adam's approaching form, led me to an understanding of how things would always be.

The hunt was its main priority. The rest was collateral damage. Even its host's sanity.

My consciousness trailed back to Adam who now stood in front of us, bloodied hand hovering over our skin. Hyde trembled with anticipation, and our shared body hummed with energy that begged for the release of a particular kind. It was a release that my love, adoration, and physical intimacy with Emmett could not satiate. Feeling how Adam enthralled her was all the evidence I needed.

After another heartbeat, Adam placed his hand on our belly. An electric zap of wanting moved through Hyde. It must have been obvious because Adam grinned, the blue of his eyes flashed with the same need she felt. He then dragged his hand across our flesh to our hip, then down to our ass, replacing the cool metal with rabid heat that penetrated every atom of our shared body.

Our breaths turned ragged, lust, peril, and unknown rage moving through us. The rage, I didn't understand. The rage left me confused.

He lifted the knife in his other hand and pressed it lightly against the skin of our neck, eyes meeting from a mere inch away. I saw a shift in his gorgeous eyes – Emmett moving behind the scenes just like I had been.

"Are you ready to meet your beast?" Adam asked, his voice a quiet growl filled with primal longing.

Through slightly parted lips, I heard Hyde whisper the only word Adam needed to hear.

"Yes."

CHAPTER SIX

Wet heat enveloped my body as the darkness of slumber surrounded me, leaving me unaware of the things that took place between Adam and Hyde. I didn't want to know, and I was certain Emmett didn't either. Of course, I was certain we would be well aware of what had transpired soon enough.

Then I heard it.

The steady beating of a human heart. Whether it was all in my head or not, I didn't know, but I could have sworn it beat inside my chest too. There was no way it was that loud without that being the case.

It grew louder and louder until I felt myself slowly come to consciousness, each neuron in my brain firing to life as if it had been hibernating. After a moment, I felt Emmett's warmth against my back, his arm draped across my side as he slept. With the awareness of him against me, also came the knowledge that my skin felt thick and sticky with something else. And it covered nearly every inch of my body and the sheets beneath us.

THE DARK OF YOU   Kindra Sowder

It also came to my realization that the heartbeat I thought I heard, was someone knocking on the door to the bedroom – mine or Emmett's, I couldn't tell. My eyes were still closed off to the world. Maybe it would be better if I remained this way as I didn't really want to see what I knew covered me from head to toe, and more than likely Emmett too.

After a few more slams on the door, I felt Emmett unwrap himself from around me, shifting in the bed to get up. He groaned, but his footfalls still slapped on the hardwood floor. His bedroom. His apartment.

No, Adam's apartment.

I could tell because of how his heels sounded hitting the solid wood of the floor that flowed through the entire home. My bedroom didn't have wood flooring at all, and Emmett's was tiled — something that could stand up to the paints he used.

The lock on the door clicked, and it creaked open. Soft mumbles greeted my ears, one voice sounding deep and familiar.

Jackson had come to see Emmett. That, or protect him from something. Who knew?

THE DARK OF YOU Kindra Sowder

I remained silent and still as they spoke, but then heard the door close and Emmett close the distance back to the bed. His hand slid up my arm and to my shoulder, giving me a subtle shake. His breath hot on my ear, he breathed softly as if to wake me slowly.

"Good morning, love. It's time we got up," he whispered.

I moaned and stirred, turning toward the warmth of his body. As I did so, I felt a slick, sticky coolness slide across my skin on the sheets. My stomach turned at the feel of it, and my eyes shot open. The room was completely dark except for what forced its way underneath the door.

"What…?" I started.

"Shhh. It's better if you don't see it. Adam and Hyde weren't exactly careful with our bodies last night. Or shy."

"I know congealed blood when I feel it, Emmett," I said as I slowly sat up, sheet peeling away from my naked back. "Whose is it?"

I felt him shrug beside me and heard a heavy sigh.

"No clue." He kissed me carefully on the shoulder. "I'll start a shower. Give me a second."

"Okay," I replied, not sure what else I could possibly say.

Before I turned my head to try to see him in the dark, he sprang from the bed and rushed into the master bath — catching a glimpse of him once the light flicked on.

Dark red had been smeared across almost every expanse of skin I spied, sending a shiver down my spine. Quickly, I squeezed my eyes shut to avoid looking at my flesh, shaking slightly with disgust and cold.

"What the fuck?" I asked in a hiss to my other self. "What did you do?"

A sharp zing ran through my mind, my eyes shot open, and I looked toward the mirror across from the bed as if she had directed me to do it without words. The ends of my hair were caked with blood, and even more of it had begun to crust over on my skin. Except the blood under the sheets with us. And it was everywhere, like they had splattered it on the bed and rolled around in it like pigs. I swallowed a gasp and fingered the ends of my bloodied hair.

THE DARK OF YOU Kindra Sowder

"What did you do?" I asked, almost sobbing.

I had a feeling it would be bad once we embraced them both together, but I never imagined this. Whatever *this* was.

"Do you really want to know?" Hyde asked, a sly, deliberate smile spreading across her lips. "Just close your pretty little eyes and wash it all away. And remember, you let this happen. You let me in and embraced me, and now you're holding up your end of the deal. So, suck it up, Blythe. You wanted it. You just didn't realize how much until I showed you everything."

The grin on her face grew even more sinister, and I couldn't look at our shared face any longer. I did as she suggested. I closed my eyes and squeezed them shut as tight as I could, realizing blood had crusted around my eyes – something I hadn't noticed seconds earlier.

I didn't expect this. Nothing – nothing – could have prepared me for this. Despite not being certain what had taken place between Adam and Hyde. They were carnal, bloody, and primal. That much I knew about them, but Hyde was unpredictable. Even Emmett had said just as much about Adam.

THE DARK OF YOU KINDRA SOWDER

Together, who knew what they were truly capable of?

I pulled air deep into my lungs and pushed it out, trying to regain some equilibrium as my stomach churned and my heart started to run a marathon in my chest.

"God, help me," I whispered to myself.

Tears stung my eyes, but I couldn't open them. There had been so much carnage. Our love was being marred by their need for violence, and it would always be that way. Somehow, now that all aspects of ourselves had found each other, we had to make that work. I just couldn't see how yet.

Solutions are for problems, Blythe. And we don't have a problem, I heard Hyde purr in my mind.

The next thing I heard was the sound of running water in the bathroom, followed by his footfalls across the floor as he neared the bed. The mattress shifted under his weight as he sat before me, placing his hands on mine that sat in my lap. He rubbed his palms over my filthy skin, flakes of blood coming off onto his palms.

"You up for a shower?" he asked quietly, almost as if he were afraid to speak to me.

I nodded but didn't speak. I couldn't. The thoughts in my head wouldn't have translated well when spoken regardless. Turmoil colored them with the crimson of the blood we had spilled.

I opened my eyes and looked into his, the same turmoil painted on his face.

"Do you have any idea who this all belongs to?" I asked, raising my arms slightly to show the dark red against my pale skin.

"I do now, yes," replied with a nod. "It's ours." He sighed heavily, rose from the bed, and held his arms out to me. "You'll see."

Shock almost stopped me from taking his hands, but morbid curiosity got the better of me. I glanced at the mirror to see my reflection nod as if to affirm the truth of his words. Looking up at him, I saw sorrow and anger in his eyes. The fact that Hyde and Adam would put us through something so uncertain seemed to bother him. Or at least, them putting me through it. I had managed for so long on my own. Now that we were moving through this together, it seemed as if Hyde was more willing to test my boundaries. We did have a deal. That our needs would be separated, but we'd give in to each other and let each other have our wants. But had she taken it too far? Only time would tell.

After a few heartbeats, I took his hands and allowed him to guide me to my feet and into the bathroom. The water coming from the showerhead was so hot steam poured from it, fogging up the entire room.

Together, we stepped into the stream of scalding liquid. I hissed at the contact on my cool skin, but it felt amazing. It would easily wash away the filth of the night before. I looked down at it, the mixture of sticky and dried blood flowing down my legs and down the drain in a swirl of crimson.

We moved in sync, forcing our bodies under the spray, and watched as our skin peaked out from underneath the life force that covered us. As my eyes took in every inch of exposed flesh, I noticed pink lines – slashes in the process of healing – covering almost every inch. He just stared at me, obviously keeping his eyes on my face instead of the rest of my body. With one slender fingertip, I traced one of the lines right below his collarbone. It was thick and angry still but fading as time went on. It had been worse. I could tell. I had seen my past injuries heal in the same fashion.

"What...?" I started, looking down at my own body as inch after inch of skin lay bare for me to witness.

"Shhh," he hushed, pulling me closer to him. "It's okay. It'll be all right."

I curled into him, laying my head on his broad chest as we stood there under the cleansing heat. If I hadn't expected something horrible before, I truly had not expected what had been unearthed in that shower. I had not expected to find the other part of me was so willing to mutilate the body we shared. She had always been keen on self-preservation. But in Adam's presence, that didn't seem to matter anymore.

She had willingly mutilated us both, and the evidence was right before my eyes.

"Shhh," Emmett continued, rubbing my back in long strokes with his fingers. "Everything will be all right."

CHAPTER SEVEN

Stifled... That was the word for what I felt as I walked into the gallery sporting a turtleneck and pants to hide the fading scars left behind by Hyde and Adam's escapades.

Autumn began to set in. That much was clear as the chill in the air nipped at my face and the leaves changed color. I hadn't noticed up until that moment, living so much in my head that the seasons barely registered as they passed.

Passing through the glass doors, I spied Lauren across the massive space, her ample cleavage on display per usual. Hannah watched over the paintings being carried toward the storeroom, pointing, and giving directions. Every few seconds, Lauren would nod and point to another painting on the wall. They were packing up from the last showing – one that Lauren was assigned lead on. From the look of the stickers on the walls, she had done Hannah and I both proud. Every painting that we absolutely hoped would sell had, from the look of it.

THE DARK OF YOU   Kindra Sowder

"Looks like it went well," I said, beaming as I approached her.

Her eyes grew wide, and she scanned me from head to toe. She was inspecting me, noticing something I hadn't when I worried about what to wear to cover up that morning.

"Hey," she replied. "It went okay."

"It went exceptionally well, Blythe. She's being humble," Hannah admonished as she stared down at us from her perch at the top of the steps to her office. "Kind of like you."

"Oh," Lauren started, rolling her eyes, "Blythe doesn't know how to be humble. She knows she's the best in New York. Hands down. Maybe even the entire community." She winked my way.

"What can I say?" I asked as I stopped beside her and gave a little shrug. "I give the people what they want."

"Especially a *certain* person," Lauren muttered, poking me in the ribs with a well-placed elbow.

"All right, all right. You've made your point," I said.

THE DARK OF YOU Kindra Sowder

Hannah turned her attention back to the movers, directing them in quick succession as her words faded into the background. Lauren turned toward me — her face etched in worry as her brows knit together. I missed something. I knew it. I had to have with the way she stared at my face.

"Are you okay? You look," she twirled her hand as she tried to think of her next word, "… tired. Emmett keeping you busy when you're not here?"

"Very," I answered honestly. "I wish I knew where he got the energy."

I knew where he got it. The same place I did. Too bad I couldn't utter a single word about it to her no matter how much I wanted to. She would never look at me the same again. That, and I was pretty certain she'd turn me in for being a serial killer. Not that they'd find the evidence. Hyde always seemed to make absolutely sure of that.

"Well," she snickered, "whatever he's taking, he needs to share. These things are fucking exhausting. I don't know how you do it all the time."

THE DARK OF YOU   Kindra Sowder

"That's why I decided it was your turn. No reason to keep all the success to myself. You're good at this. You just need to get your hands dirty."

She sighed, turning to me with obvious bags under her made-up eyes. It was clear she had attempted to cover them up, but it didn't take much to see she had too much fun – and booze – the night before.

"I mean, a good time was had by all. I just wish it didn't come with an exhausting price tag."

"Join the club," I said, tapping a finger under my eye.

"No. That's one place I will not be joining tonight. This bitch needs some beauty rest," she said as her hand went up to her face, touching the puffy area just underneath her right eye. "Fuck," she muttered. "Well, at least I don't have to worry about anyone dropping in here today. Everyone will be scheduling their appointments to pick these things up, and all that can be done over the phone. Just have to make the calls."

"And that, my dear, sweet friend, is the easiest part," I replied.

THE DARK OF YOU KINDRA SOWDER

"Just know," Hannah nearly shouted as she came down the steps toward us, finally done bossing the movers around, "it gets easier, darling. Much easier. At some point," she stopped at the base of the steps, untucking a newspaper from under her arm, "you'll learn when to put the wine glass down. No matter how much money they're willing to spend."

She waved it in the air, a look of trepidation on her face.

"What's that?" Lauren asked.

"Just news of the latest, greatest serial killer, dear. We hadn't heard anything for a while, but looks like their investigation is ramping up," she answered, practically shoving the newspaper in my direction.

"Is that so?" I asked, eyes skeptical. "I figured they would have caught him by now."

I knew better. Much better. They hadn't caught me and Hyde in our disgusting tirade over the years – they weren't about to catch Emmet and Adam in theirs either.

"Do you think they'll catch him?" I asked, eyes glancing at the front page.

THE DARK OF YOU Kindra Sowder

The Ripper of New York Continues Rampage.

I almost rolled my eyes as I saw the photos of his victims, registering each face as completely recognizable before squaring my jaw, dropping the shocked expression, and looking to Hannah as if I were unaware of who they spoke of. I couldn't talk. My inner demon was just more careful about things than his. Of course, they didn't seem to have much evidence to find and ID the killer from what little I knew of things.

"I don't think so. They have nothing. That headline is to grab attention. To bring in readers. A ridiculous effort to boost sales. It's all a charade, dear. They have nothing new," Hannah admitted.

But I did.

As I watched their expressions change from amusement to horror, I had more evidence of Emmett's involvement than anyone. I had just never realized it until that moment. How I had never recognized the faces in the newspaper before, I couldn't even begin to fathom. Every cell in my body hummed and buzzed with what felt like a thousand bees moving underneath my skin.

Anxiety.

My heart raced, heat licking up my belly and into my chest as I swallowed down the panic that began to creep through me. I had missed it. Just like so many others. Those same people who missed something so particularly important now had proof hanging in their homes.

I held the paper up and waved it a little.

"Can I borrow this?"

"Absolutely. Keep it. I don't usually read the news, anyway," Hannah said as she turned and walked toward the back of the gallery toward where the movers went as she directed them. "Back to work!"

We watched Hannah walk away for a moment. I stood there frozen in place as my arm fell to my side, paper still in hand. My body swayed slightly as my next step for the day solidified in my mind.

"Hey," Lauren whispered, as if trying not to startle me.

I turned to her, concern painting her features as her brow furrowed and she frowned.

"Hmmm?" I asked, my eyebrows popping up.

THE DARK OF YOU Kindra Sowder

"Are you okay?" she asked. "You're pale. Are you sick?"

"No," I replied, shaking my head. "I'm okay. Just a lot on my mind, is all. I'll be fine once I get some work done. Get my mind on other things."

"Right," she said, as if she knew what work lay ahead.

I had a few things to look into – make sure my memory served me well enough. I was certain I had seen those faces before, and I had sold them in this very gallery. A part of me had known it all along. A part of me that, while divulging so much to me, still held many secrets.

How could I have not seen it before?

CHAPTER EIGHT

As I sat at my desk tucked away in a small office I hardly ever used, the faces of Adam's victims stared back at me. I knew they were his victims. They had to be. He and I were the only ones of our kind to run amuck through New York City like this.

If there were more, they remained hidden extremely well. Better than even I had. If I didn't cause a stir at all, there was no way Adam would have figured out who and what I was. Unless he had been keeping an eye out specifically for others like him, scouring the archives, family genealogies and histories, as well as police reports and files.

Of course, one of my ancestors was in his book. And it wasn't as if my immediate family didn't have major serial killer vibes. They did. My parents sacrificed themselves for what they thought was a supernatural gift. That wasn't the case, no matter what Cyra said before telling me about Adam. We were created by forces beyond the natural, that much was clear, but not in the way my parents believed. I really needed to sit down and read the entirety of that book. Once I did, I would likely know as much as I needed to. Even if I still have questions, I may have the right pathways to find the answers.

Now, as I looked at these women's smiling faces peering up from the newsprint, I couldn't help but shiver at the known ways they met their ultimate demises. Ripped apart by Adam's hands while Emmett likely watched in the background of his shared mind unable to stop the violence and bloodlust from taking place. Adam likely used them for his own sinister sexual needs only to destroy any hopes and dreams they may have had before the end of the carnality ended. The reflex to wretch tried to force its way past my gag reflex, but I swallowed it down with an ice-cold cup of coffee that had started out piping hot.

Reaching down, I opened one of the deep drawers and rifled through the mountain of catalogs inside. I held onto one from each show I put together – a track record of my life's work. Artists ranging from abstract to realist passed through my fingertips until I found what I was looking for.

The one from Emmett's most recent showing came into view, and I snapped it up, eyeing the name boldly printed across the tab in black marker and shutting the drawer with a harsh thud in one swift movement.

I placed it down on the desk, my eyes going back and forth between the newspaper and the small simple catalog. My heart raced as the thought of opening it roared through my mind, making me wonder how much I honestly wanted to know if Emmett painted Adam's victims. And if he did, was it to help process the losses of these women in his human mind? Or as a trophy for his demon's enjoyment? Or both?

I sat there for a moment before finally turning the first page open, the fourth victim out of twenty greeting me in shades of a ravishing purple. Almost royal. Her face looked amazed, almost worshipping.

"Fuck," I whispered.

I turned to the next page, seeing the seventh victim in emerald green. Her expression showed the same as the first in the catalog. They were amazed by him – not afraid of him. Which told me they were being seen through Emmett's eyes. I knew that, even if it were me on the surface looking back down at them, Hyde was always there looking down with me. There was no way around that, and nothing could ever change it. Not even a deal with the Devil.

As that thought crossed my mind, I felt Hyde stir within her recesses of the darkened corners of my very soul, rippling through my mind as she forced her way to the surface.

It's never just you, Blythe. Never has been. Not since you were born, I felt the words roll through my brain like they were whispered in my ear.

"You've done nothing but ruin my life," I hissed, tapping my finger on the page of the catalog. "You and Adam both. This links us to the killer, you dipshit."

I had never taken that tone with Hyde before. I had always been too scared – too… *fragile.* I felt her recoil in my mind and then felt a sinister smile spread across my lips that wasn't on purpose, nor controllable.

"Our life, you mean," she said before the doorknob leading into the office jiggled slightly.

As quickly as I could, I shoved the catalog in my lap and opened the paper to the first, most unassuming page I could find – settling in as if I had been there just reading the sports section. Out of my peripheral vision, I saw a flash of pink hair shining in the LED light above my head. A strong scent came in with her, smelling like chemicals and plastic. Acrylic paint. The smell almost completely covered up the floral-scented perfume she wore, and the mixture was nauseating.

Raising my eyes to meet hers, she was dressed in a black tank top, and a nice pair of slacks – probably wearing heels. That seemed to be typical for her unless she was in her studio. Like she was trying to impress those outside those confines despite that fact I could easily spot the stain of black acrylic on the fabric that covered her and the smear of crimson she missed on the underside of her right wrist.

"Look who decided to grace me with her presence," I said, smirking.

Her eyes locked on mine, the expression on her face bleeding with contempt. The smirk never left my lips. Since our last conversation, which I felt left on a rather threatening note, I hadn't wanted much to do with her. Plus, since she finally showed her true colors to me, everything had changed.

Once I knew exactly who Emmett was, the reality of Cyra came into crystal-clear focus.

She approached the desk and leaned forward, placing her hands on the desk's surface just inches from the edge of the newspaper I had been pretending to read.

"Well, Blythe, I wouldn't have to if we didn't have a little problem," she said, tapping an unmanicured nail on the wood. I looked down at her tapping with contempt only to notice the stains of paint within the cuticle. I looked back up to her, meeting her eyes and locking in my serious tone for whatever she had to say next.

"And *what* is this *problem,* Cyra?" I asked, tilting my head to the side.

"You really don't know?" she asked with a sigh.

"Know what?" I asked, pulling the catalog off of my lap, and practically slamming it on the desk. "Did I know that every single one of Emmett's paintings… the ones that I sold mind you… was basically an admission of guilt for each and every one of Adam's victims? That he's the serial killer they've been looking for? That now, those women are hanging in unsuspecting people's homes?"

"No, Blythe. I mean, I knew you'd figure that out eventually, but there's another problem," she said as she stood, crossing her arms over her chest. "That cop that came sniffing around your apartment. He'll be coming back. I saw it." With her index finger, she tapped on her left temple, indicating yet another vision had come to her.

"Those visions are bullshit, Cyra. We both know it. You haven't seen shit. You just worked for Adam the entire time. You had insight. Not premonitions. Don't play games with me anymore. I'm tired of them. You know he's coming back just like me and Emmett do. Because this cop smells something. Any good cop can smell something foul when he sees it."

"You're not concerned?" she asked.

"While this does link me in a lot of ways to Adam's *extracurricular* activities, and Emmett would take the fall for it all, I can't say that I am. I've covered my tracks well over the years. Well," I paused, "Hyde has. I get locked up, so does she. Adam doesn't seem to think along the same lines as she does. And Emmett deserves some sort of grieving process for those women. I had always just hoped I wouldn't be the one to attract it, despite what I know karma has coming for me because of Hyde."

"And?" she pushed.

THE DARK OF YOU KINDRA SOWDER

I sighed as I shrugged.

"I hoped I was just making connections where there weren't any. Turns out, I knew all along on some level. Just didn't want to admit it to myself. But it doesn't matter. At any rate, this conversation is over. Our last conversation told me exactly *who* you are. You don't need to act like you're worried for me. You're just wanting to cover your ass to keep your meal ticket going. That's all."

She huffed and crossed her arms over her chest, anger and knowing etched on her face.

"There's a lot more behind all of this than you think. You'd know that if you *actually* read more of the book Adam gave you. I suggest, before you go riding around on your high horse too much, you read more of it."

"I already know about my ancestor, Cyra. I know…"

"You know zilch, psycho. Read the goddamned book as soon as you get home," she said as she moved toward the door, reaching her hand out and taking the knob in her hand. She turned back to me, raised an eyebrow, and grinned – as if accusing me of something.

"When that detective is done with you, of course. You'll be seeing him shortly."

"You think I'm going to sell him out, don't you?" I asked.

"I don't know," she paused. "Are you?"

I shook my head.

"No. I never even considered it. Plus, even if I did and they had enough evidence to arrest him, how long do you think they'd survive him? I'm sure they wouldn't make it out the door in one piece. Adam wouldn't allow that."

"They wouldn't catch him. They wouldn't get the chance. He's been around too long to not have learned a few things. He's been slashing a bloody path through history for over two thousand years. A weak beat cop won't be able to stop him," Cyra stated.

"You're probably right," I replied with a nod. "We'll just have to see how this all pans out, I guess."

She chuckled and opened the door, leaving without saying a word. She did at least shut the door behind her when she exited. That in itself was a small relief as I needed a brief moment to myself without anyone just walking by and seeing how pissed off Cyra could make me with her sheer presence.

It wasn't the conversation I imagined having. Not anywhere near the level of evil I expected considering the last time we spoke. My mind started to race at the thought of what could have changed things so drastically I'd notice. It had to be the threat to Emmett. That had to be it.

It didn't matter, in the end, though. None of it did. In the end, I stood between Emmett, Adam, and the legal system. Not that it could ever hold him.

Leaning forward, I placed my elbows on the desk and rubbed my temples with my fingertips. A migraine was starting – something I hadn't experienced in years. Somehow, with Hyde along for the ride, I had managed to avoid the level of stress it usually took to trigger one. The pressure building and throbbing on the left side of my head would continue until I was debilitated. An aura passed over my vision, kind of like electric static that went away just as quickly as it came.

"This is so not what I need right now," I groaned. "Damn that little bitch."

I felt Hyde within as if she were in complete agreeance of my assessment of Cyra.

A knock on my closed door broke the silence, pulling my attention slightly away from the pain in my head.

"Yeah?" I asked, barely looking up from the grain of the desk.

I heard the door open, and another pair of heels entered the room.

"Cyra," I jerked in response, "he's a …"

When I looked up, I saw Hannah standing there with concern in her eyes, brows furrowed. I truly hadn't expected to see her when I looked up.

"Oh, Hannah. I'm sorry. I've just got a migraine coming," I started to explain.

"No need to say anything, dear," she said, raising her hand. "I just wish you told me you were in some sort of trouble."

Confusion blossomed in my chest, my face scrunching and my brows knotting together.

"What do you mean? I'm not in any kind of… trouble," I answered.

99

THE DARK OF YOU   Kindra Sowder

As I said the words, Detective Bell entered the room – looming in the doorway as his eyes met mine. They were cold – dark – showing he knew nothing and felt nothing. As if trying not to give away the reason for his visit. The bags under his eyes from obvious fatigue only intensified his stare. Like most officers in the great city of New York, overworked, underpaid, and not appreciated. Under the circumstances though, the last one I felt was justified. I did not wish to see nor speak to him about anything he was sniffing around but yet, here he was.

I already knew what he would say before he uttered a single word. Hannah had stepped aside to allow the man into my office. His words made her show me something I had never seen her show before. Concern.

"Miss McAllister," he said, voice deep and gravelly with exhaustion. "I'm going to need you to come with me to the station. I have some questions I think only you can answer."

CHAPTER NINE

Not even thirty minutes later, I sat in the dark, dingy interrogation room at whatever precinct I was brought to – tapping my fingernails on the surface of the grimy metal table. Scratches marred its lackluster surface, and I could tell it had never been thoroughly cleaned. At least, not with anything more than just water and a paper towel. I cringed and pulled my arms into my lap, goosebumps forming underneath the turtleneck I wore.

I was certain they kept it cold in there for a reason. To make you feel more of a sense of impending doom. It was also why they made you wait for them to come talk to you after coming to your door and making it sound as if it was of the utmost importance. They wanted to watch you squirm, but I wouldn't be giving them the satisfaction. Living with Hyde my entire life, I became an expert at not showing my fear or anxiety.

I also became an expert at hiding my guilt.

Anything that could incriminate me, or anyone else for that matter, would not come out of my mouth. No matter what he said.

101

THE DARK OF YOU   KINDRA SOWDER

Hyde rolled around inside me, clenching deep in my gut as I continued to swallow down the unease that came with sitting in that room. While I may be an expert at hiding it from the outside world, inside I had to remember to keep calm. The detective knew how to make someone squirm, that was for sure. The apprehension I felt had me picking my fingernails, which I hadn't done in years.

Don't fidget, Hyde whispered in my head, nearly inaudible. *It'll make you look guilty of something. Let's not give them any fuel to start a fire with whatever twigs they've gathered, shall we?*

Of course, she would make an appearance when I couldn't respond but unfortunately, she had a very good point and I stopped picking my fingernails.

You're even more annoying when I can't actually yell at you, you know?, I thought at her.

Silence greeted me, but I knew she seethed inside. I felt her desire to come out, but she was well aware we were in a precarious circumstance, and I needed to keep control.

Just as the thought crossed my mind, there was an audible click and the door swung open, revealing the detective. His cheap suit clung to him in all the wrong places. I had no doubt there was a decent enough physique underneath. He smiled at me softly as if trying to reassure me everything would be fine, but I had a strong suspicion it wouldn't be.

Not even close.

I returned the grin with clenched teeth, my jaw aching slightly with the tension.

"Miss McAllister, sorry about the wait," he apologized with a somewhat jovial tone. "Wife called, complaining about the kids. Well, anyway... I apologize."

He was lying. I took a quick look at his hands and there was no ring on his finger, nor a tan line from where one would be. Even so, I decided to play along with his little game. Although, I couldn't stop the eye roll that came at his statement.

"Not like I had anything else to do," I said flatly.

He didn't respond, only sat down in the uncomfortable chair matching mine across the table from me, and unbuttoned his suit jacket. His eyes scanned me as we both sat there and stared at one another. My heart raced, but I gave no hint of the turmoil I felt knowing any question he asked me, the answer would most likely be a lie. I couldn't just protect myself anymore. Emmett and Adam could not fall into the hands of the police. Not just because of my feelings for Emmett, but for the protection of anyone who crossed Adam's path. I silently told myself to calm down in my mind.

"I *am* sorry about pulling you from work. You looked busy," he apologized.

"It's the art world, Detective. I'm always busy. Rich people with too much money to dcal with," I stated sarcastically. "You said you had some questions for me?"

"Down to business," he chuckled.

"Always," I replied.

"Right," he said with a nod, leaning forward and placing his arms on the disgusting table. "This is about…"

"The man I slept with? Yeah, I had a feeling. What else could I possibly tell you that I haven't already?"

"Are you certain that's the last time you saw him?" he asked, eyebrows furrowed as if already frustrated.

"One hundred percent. I don't like repeat performances," I responded as I crossed my arms over my chest.

Instantly, I knew where the next line of questioning was going. All because, as anyone now knew, that was no longer true. Emmett and I had plenty of encores within the last few weeks. I mentally kicked myself but didn't change my expression.

"Is that so?" he asked, grinning.

Shit, I thought, *he had me.*

I sat there in complete silence. If he wanted to be in control, I'd let him be as far as I was comfortable. Except, he wasn't really in control. His slightly cocky attitude seemed to be his downfall. He had met his match with me, and we would see how long he lasted.

"What about Emmett Adler?" he asked, leaning forward and placing his elbows back on the table between us.

"Ah," I said with a nod. "I take it you've been watching me, Detective. Isn't that a form of police harassment? Should I contact my attorney?"

"Well… not exactly, Miss McAllister. Of course you are not under arrest, nor in any trouble. And you can of course end this right now and contact your attorney, but I would hope you will hear me out first. While I have been watching you it had nothing to do with you to start with" he said with a nod. "The man I'm looking for, he was the last to go missing before you two… Mr. Adler, and yourself… started… ummm," he looked down toward his shirt pocket and then, thumbed through a pocket notebook he pulled from his shirt pocket and opened to a specific page, then looked up at me again, "dating. You don't find that a tad odd? I mean, for someone who claims to only enjoy the one night fling with no repeats."

"Are you insinuating he was the last victim because I found someone long-term?" I probed.

"I didn't say you killed anyone, Miss McAllister. I am just trying to make sense of where this missing person is and how he became a file on my desk at the end of my shift one night. Something is not adding up, Miss McAllister, and I am very hopeful you can shed some light on this and help me out." He placed the notepad back in his pocket.

"Blythe," I stated firmly. "Everyone knows the only reason you detail anyone is if you believe in a theory, Detective. I'm not some stupid little schoolgirl you can get one over on."

"I never said you were," he stated.

"You don't have to. A lot of you think alike. You think I did something. I'd just like to know what kind of evidence you think you have. Plus, you said he's missing. Not dead. So, I'm inclined to think the spoiled rich boy took off somewhere on a bender."

"So, you knew him well?" the detective asked.

"Not at all," I said as I shook my head. "Like I said, one-night stand. Found him, fucked him, forgot him. He left my apartment, and I have not seen him since. As far as the spoiled rich boy statement, you can always tell the type. I grew up around enough of them."

Detective Bell sat there another moment, studying me. After a couple of silent seconds, he reached into his suit jacket and produced a manilla envelope that I hadn't noticed. Placing it on the table, he opened it and began removing what looked like photos from inside it, turning them so I could see the images.

The first I saw was a color photo of me leaving my apartment for a night out with Lauren, but the next I hadn't expected. Detective Bell placed it down on the table on top of my own image, smirking slightly.

I chose not to react as I spotted a very familiar face in the next photo – Lauren and I walking down the street smiling with Emmett lurking behind us. His eyes blazed with something nearly unrecognizable if I hadn't seen it before.

Lust and rage all mixed together. Something I saw move through Emmett's face when Adam attempted to force himself to the surface.

"Did you know your boyfriend had been stalking you, Blythe?" the detective asked, genuine concern creeping into his voice as I stared at the photo.

He produced another photo, then another, and another until there was a small stack of them from various outings sitting there on the table between us. Even some at the gallery and leaving my apartment building. Before that moment, I knew Emmett had more information on me than anyone should have. I had been as careful as possible in my line of work, and in the amount of cash that padded my trust fund. But I never realized it had been that extensive.

That made me wonder. Was it Emmett or Adam that housed the dark obsession – if not both?

The detective must have taken my silence as an admission of ignorance because he took a deep breath in front of me and placed one large hand on my wrist. Shortly after, he showed me to a patrol car that would return me to the gallery. The whole trip back I only thought of one thing. How could I have been so blind?

I had been ignorant of many things, but this had not been one of them. I knew he had been on some level. I just never considered how deep that obsession went until that moment as I stared at photo after photo. Each one he mostly wore the same expression I had seen in the first the detective showed me. In a few, I saw the emotions behind Emmett's intentions – love fueled by need. What the need was, I wasn't sure, but I'd have to find out somehow.

Then it hit me. I had an entire box filled with documents provided by the very man – creature – that followed me for weeks before our meeting. Prior to me selling his paintings. Every part of my body turned hot,

109

Hyde rolling inside as if nodding like she had had that information all along. She had been busy hiding a lot of things despite our agreement, but there were two sides to that arrangement, and she was allowing me to have what I requested.

No matter the price.

CHAPTER TEN

Nothing made sense to me anymore as I sat on the floor surrounded by documents and books containing the history of my bloodline – including Adam's origins. I had known extraordinarily little from what I had gleaned before, but this was far beyond the scope of what I had expected. His history spanned more than two thousand years.

But my lineage seemed to come from nothing – just appeared.

I pulled the massive bound book back into my lap, the image of the statue Adam kept in his special room on the page. The color was so brilliant it almost illuminated on the page just like it did in our presence. Sitting there with legs crossed in the middle of my living room floor, I stared at the page for a few moments. My mind raced as I thought, remembering how the statue – so primal and beautiful – glowed brilliantly and then its light intensified as our blood was shed in that room.

THE DARK OF YOU KINDRA SOWDER

Hyde rolled within as if reacting to those images. Of course, she was. She always reacted to anything having to do with bloodshed.

That… and Adam.

With a sigh, I closed my eyes and rubbed my temples in frustration. Gaps in my memory did not help me figure things out. Hyde had done an excellent job at hiding things from me that she felt would be traumatizing, which led me to believe she had always been there – even in childhood. Massive lapses of time left blank spaces where there shouldn't have been, and the documents and book before me did little to help fill any of those cracks and crevices.

Hyde remained silent as I sat there except for the butterflies she always lent my way when she stirred as a constant reminder she was lurking just beneath the surface.

I raked my hands through my hair and looked back down at the page, completely perplexed. I knew Adam's story. Emmet had given me everything. Well, as far as I knew. Knowing Hyde could keep things deep down in the dark recesses of my mind that I couldn't access, I would have imagined Adam could do the same – if not more extensively.

THE DARK OF YOU Kindra Sowder

"Why do you guys have to make this so goddamned hard?" I asked the empty air.

I sat there for another moment, attempting to decipher everything I just read. It wasn't like it was a foreign language or anything but my mind could not wrap around the actuality of the words in black and white. The thought hit me again. We originated with Adam as a whole, but my particular line just appeared seemingly out of nowhere. But, how? That simple fact would explain why Adam was so mystified and intrigued by me... and, of course... Hyde. Him and Emmett had been watching us for quite a while. That much was also clear among the handwritten notes and photos that I also discovered in the box. Apparently, much longer than the good detective had noticed and recorded himself.

That brought my mind back to the statue. From what I had been told, and what I gleaned out of the massive book, it was used in the ceremony that Pythagoras and his group performed to create Adam – among others. That led me to know that Adam was not indeed the first but from a smaller and stronger line.

Something made him special. Something set him apart.

THE DARK OF YOU Kindra Sowder

That was what made him the first, but I was confused as to what *that* even was. He seemed to function a lot like Hyde and myself, but Adam did exhibit more control over Emmett. They didn't seem to work together like we had. We came to an accord of sorts, while Emmett and Adam struggled. So much so that Adam went unchecked, leaving bodies in alleyways with their hearts ripped out of their chests.

Maybe it was the statue itself that changed something in him as if the statue could pick and choose traits of an individual to reconstruct. Or it was something in the genes that reacted to the effects of the stone. From what little I knew about where it came from, it was carved from some ancient rock. The book told me that much, but maybe there was more to it. Maybe I was missing something entirely that wasn't in the book or any of the documents surrounding me. I just, for the life of me, could not figure out what that could possibly be or where to begin to search for answers. I had thought I would find more within these writings but that hasn't panned out as a full ideal situation either.

At the moment the thought crossed my mind, a jolt of recollection zapped through my brain. A sharp pain penetrated my forehead right behind my eyes as the image flashed in the recesses of my memory. I only knew it was a memory because it felt familiar.

My heart raced as I felt Hyde unfurl like a wolf inside my deepest and most repressed memories. She snapped and snarled as it surfaced again, as if her animal ferocity would help to bring it forward.

To help me remember.

Then I was completely immersed.

I stood before my parents at the tender age of seven, surrounded by what I noticed was the inside of a bank vault lined with safe deposit boxes. Everything felt real, as if I were standing there in that exact moment instead of a memory.

My mother's red hair stood out amongst the white walls, twisted into a bun at the nape of her neck — her slender body sheathed in a nice black dress while my father wore a blue suit and power tie. I remembered his shoes gleaming in the fluorescent lights – just shined and buffed that morning. His typical routine.

Another man stood before them, dressed in a gray pin-stripe suit and blue tie. His face looked solemn as his large hand placed a key into a lock on one of the silver boxes and turned it, his lip twitching and causing his salt and pepper mustache to move with it. I remembered wanting to giggle at his expression but remained silent. My parents had made it clear I was to be seen and not heard while inside.

The man turned the key, and I heard the click of the lock inside echo off the vault's walls. In one swift movement, he turned and placed the large lockbox on a table I had just noticed though I was eye-level with its surface. I watched as he opened the lid but could not see what was housed inside. From what little I knew at that age — I knew only important things were kept in boxes like those.

"Do you have the item?" he asked, his voice somewhat hoarse with nervousness.

"Of course," my mother stated, turning to reach inside the large purse hanging off her shoulder.

As she fished for a moment, the man looked down at me and smiled softly, the wrinkles at the corners of his eyes became more pronounced as his youthful look was starting to fade into a middle-aged man. I remembered smiling back at him. It had been nice to be acknowledged even though what we were doing wasn't particularly for me.

After a few seconds, she removed a large blue felt jewelry box from her purse. She opened it to inspect its contents, giving me a small peek as to what was inside. A beautiful necklace gleamed under the lights – a lovely deep green stone sparkling at the base surrounded by what looked to be diamonds that joined at the top. Silver clasps were joined at what would be the tip of the stones as though they were held in place by small pieces of fabric.

It was stunning, but I held my tiny gasp in.

Her eyes shifted to look up at my father, an unknown question in them I couldn't decipher. He nodded, his gaze penetrating though he wasn't looking at me. My parents always had a bond deeper than most I had seen growing up – into my teenage years I learned why.

She closed the box and handed it to the man, who swiftly placed it in the safe deposit box and locked it – precious cargo, now secure from prying eyes. My little mind raced as I watched the exchange, curiosity begging to be released. I watched for a moment as the box was placed back into the wall of the vault. As soon *as he turned the key and the lock clicked, he looked at me and I saw the forlorn look in his eyes.*

And just like that, my awareness seemed to slam back into my body.

The massive breath that forcibly entered my lungs burned so badly that I couldn't keep the cough from erupting. My entire body lunged forward, my hands catching me before I fell face-first onto the floor. I wasn't certain how long I had been like that retching like I had been holding my breath the entire time, but it had been long enough for my body to ache and ribs to spasm painfully. Bile mixed with stomach acid burned its way up my throat, but I swallowed it down. Every part of my body reacted violently to the onslaught of the memory.

Had I repressed this memory, or had Hyde done it for me? With the current state of my brain, it was far too difficult to tell.

Once my body quieted, my mind raced even more. Where was this safe deposit box? Why was this necklace so important that Hyde showed the memory buried in my mind since childhood? I had no recollection of this event prior, or I would have taken everything out of it long ago.

THE DARK OF YOU   Kindra Sowder

I rocked back on my heels, the burning quieting as I thought to myself for what felt like hours. In reality, it had only been a couple of minutes. Everything moved in slow motion as I racked my mind for information that had to be hidden there. Then I realized something. My parents left me a sizable fortune, only seemingly leaving their financial affairs to one place. One place they always trusted and I knew.

When the realization hit, I scrambled to my feet and made a beeline to my financial statements, my body instinctively knowing where to go. I kept it all in the guest room, the only person ever staying there being Lauren whom I knew I could always trust not to snoop around. She was more direct and would just ask before opening anything. Besides, she was typically too drunk from massive amounts of wine when she stayed here.

The small dark gray file cabinet came into sight as soon as I entered the simple cream guest room, my vision tunneling. I had never taken a moment to actually remember what financial institution all my money was trusted to – maybe I should have. Yanking the bottom drawer open, I pulled out the first file I saw and quickly removed one of the statements from within, revealing the name of the next place I needed to go that could give me more answers.

Hochstedler and Associates sounded too much like an attorney's office, but they happened to be one of the best banks to leave a considerable sum of money and assets with. My parents had chosen well considering how much had been left to me, and I continued to bank with them since. Granted, I hardly remembered their name on a good day, but my murderous alter ego assumed a lot of head space. And she wasn't easy to ignore.

My heart skipped a beat once my gaze met the black text, and I knew where I was headed next.

CHAPTER ELEVEN

As I entered the building, I couldn't believe I had never stepped foot in the bank before. I chose to handle everything by phone or email where allowed. Confronting the place was difficult since my parents passed.

Now, there was no choice but to. The massive lobby was white, modern, and glaring – two gigantic windows above the row of tellers before glaring down at me as if they knew what all I had done. I knew that wasn't the case, but guilt had racked me so hard it felt like every stare was an accusation.

Taking a deep, steadying breath, I pulled my thoughts to the scene in front of me. Each teller dressed in a suit ranging from charcoal grays to navy blues – every man and woman perfectly manicured and crisp. Like new money. The breath did nothing to calm my nerves, but it did give me the resolve to get my feet moving. I approached one of the tellers, her deep brown eyes matching her dark skin perfectly. Her sleek nose coupled with her hair slicked back into a pristine bun gave her an air of aristocracy.

THE DARK OF YOU   Kindra Sowder

I looked down at my disheveled self, realizing I had bolted out of my apartment in what I had been wearing – a beat-up hoodie and black leggings.

"Fuck" I said under my breath.

It could always be worse, I heard Hyde giggle in my head. *You could have come in a nightie or a bloodied bra and thong.* She internally snickered at my uneasiness of which I was not amused.

I looked up, spying my reflection in the glass that separated myself and the teller. A snide smirk twisted my lips into something almost unrecognizable, eyes filled with knowing.

"Shut up," I chided through gritted teeth.

The woman behind the glass cleared her throat, pulling my attention from my reflection. My glance jerked to her face, eyes meeting hers and holding her gaze. They held judgment – the same accusation as others before. All except Emmett and Lauren, though she seemed to be suspicious of something on occasion.

Choosing to ignore it as my gut wrenched and Hyde continued to giggle, I breezed past it and gave her my best, most professional smile. It felt forced, stretching the corners of my mouth past capacity.

"Hello, Ma'am," the woman said, a slight hint of a Swiss accent to her voice. "How may I assist you today?"

Considering the origins of the bank, I was still taken aback by the fact she even had an accent at all, but her German dialect was coming through as clearly *High German*. My language professor would be proud of me for even knowing that. I shook my head, clearing the cobwebs of surprise and the lingering effects of my repressed memory as déjà vu started to set in.

"Ummm," I started, fumbling over my words as I approached.

For fuck's sake, Blythe. Pull it together, Hyde quietly whispered inside my head in her most sincerely chiding tone.

I felt the vibrations inside me as she threatened to take over, but I swallowed, pushing her back down into the depths where she belonged.

"Yes, thank you," I said, squaring my shoulders. "I am here to pull the contents of a safe deposit box, please."

"Alright," the woman said. "Do you have the safe deposit box number?"

I mentally kicked myself. Of all the things I still could not remember, it had to be that. One of the most important things from that newly surfaced memory, and I still managed to keep that repressed. I pushed around in my mind for it, but Hyde was not obliging. I had pushed her down far enough that she seemed to get the hint and was pouting in her own dark corner in my subconscious. Not like her in the slightest, but I had to take the moments of silence where I could get them, I suppose.

I folded my hands on the marble countertop before me and tilted my head slightly in an attempt to look unassuming.

"No, I don't. But I do have the name," I explained.

"Okay, that'll do," she said with a furrowed brow, her fingers moving on the keyboard of the computer before her. "What is the name?"

"McAllister. Emile and David McAllister," I answered.

Her fingers stopped moving across the keys almost immediately, her eyes flashing up to mine in an instant. She seemed almost startled as she stared at me, nearly awestruck. I looked her in the eye, unwavering as I tried to decipher her reaction. I couldn't before she responded.

"I'll be back with you shortly. Please, have a seat and someone will come escort you in a moment," she stated, motioning toward the plush chairs off to the side of the lobby. "Is there anything I can get you while you wait? Coffee? Tea? Water?"

"No, that's okay," I replied with a shake of my head. "That's not necessary. Thank you."

"Okay, we'll be with you in a moment, then," she stated before turning on her heel and walking away, quickly.

I watched her carefully as she disappeared behind a black door behind the counter, not even taking one look back at me as she nearly sprinted toward it. Confusion racked my brain, and doubt made it easier for Hyde to resurface. It always did. I felt her unfurl as I pulled away from the counter and moved to sit in one of the black chairs that looked soft as clouds. When I sat, it enveloped my body, but I kept my back stick straight. I couldn't let my confusion about the situation make me look like I didn't belong.

THE DARK OF YOU Kindra Sowder

That was some reaction, wasn't it? She almost looked... Hyde began.

"Scared," I finished. "Scared and deified. Like she was looking into the eyes of God."

Or the Devil, Hyde growled inside my skull.

I smirked. Hyde had a very valid point, and I couldn't stop the subtle nod of my head that accompanied the grin. The Devil was more like it – sinister and cunning. But never the liar. No. Hyde and Satan did have that in common. They always told the truth. Brutal to a point but it was the truth, nonetheless.

I always wondered how Hyde managed to swing that when she emerged. Of course, it was always possible she lied to everyone else and just not to me. Then that made me wonder how many more dark moments I had that I didn't remember. I shook the thought away. I didn't want to know. I didn't need to know. She had her privacy in some instances, and I had mine. There was no way I cared to remember anything she did while I was pushed under the water of my subconscious.

With a sigh, I pulled up the sleeve of the hoodie I wore to expose the face of my watch, looking at the time. It had only been a few minutes, but it felt like it had been much longer.

My nerves started to fray as I sat there, and my legs began to shake as I looked around the expansive bank. Only a few people littered the lobby aside from the three of four employees, each not paying any attention to me. It didn't matter. I still felt like all eyes were on me, especially after seeing the woman's reaction to hearing my parent's names.

My eyes drifted to the floor – white and gray marble covered in a decently sized gray carpet that matched the lines in the marble perfectly. They must have paid the decorator well. The sleek modern lines within the space spoke of sophistication and old money, much unlike the attire I showed up in. I mentally kicked myself for a second time. I should have changed before coming here, but it was too late now.

"Ms. McAllister," a voice I recognized barged into my headspace.

My gaze shot up to find a much older version of the man in my memory standing before me, wearing a similar modernized suit and the same hairstyle. Not much had changed except for the deep creases at his eyes and mouth from years of customer service and the moustache was no longer salt and peppered but full white.

"Yes," I said as I shot to my feet. "That's me."

His eyes met mine instantly, searching my soul as those eyes bore into me. I almost curled into myself to hide but remained stoic. I felt Hyde move within me. As if he saw it himself, a smirk took residence on his lips. I saw his ribs move as he took a deep breath. I felt the urge to do the same to steady the beast within and reclaim complete control. It wouldn't have worked if I gave into it.

"I've been waiting for you, Blythe McAllister," he said very matter-of-factly. "We all have."

I swallowed hard, unsure of how to respond. Deep down, as Hyde rolled inside me once more as if welcomed by his words, I knew it to be true.

CHAPTER TWELVE

"I'm Mr. Segerson. I am the account manager for the safe deposit boxes. I am well aware of your parent's unique needs and was assigned to their particular case while you were just a child," the older man explained as he guided me through a labyrinth of hallways.

He had begun by taking me to a door I had not noticed toward the back of the lobby, perfectly hidden away from prying eyes by a rather large partition that blended in well. You'd only know of it if you worked for the bank or had an account. The door was marked *private*, and to the right of it was a slot for a key card. I had zoned out when he inserted it, only truly paying attention to his actions once we crossed the threshold. We came to an elevator door where he inserted his card and punched in a code, awaited a green light to illuminate as the doors opened. We stepped inside the elevator and the doors shut once he pushed the L1 button. He began speaking again.

"As I'm sure you're well aware, your parents had special requirements," he assumed. We started to move down quickly coming to a stop several seconds later where the doors opened into the vault. I followed him into the room. It was just as my memory suggested. Completely unchanged by time.

"Actually," I answered, "I didn't really know this deposit box existed. Their death was so sudden I guess they didn't have time to make sure this was in their wills."

"Hmmm," Mr. Segerson seemed to ponder. "How did you find out about it? It's remarkably interesting that you didn't know since your name is listed as the beneficiary of said box."

"I'm more concerned as to why your institution never contacted me about it since my trust is housed here as well," I made sure to point out. "How can it be that you never reached out to me about it?"

"Not reaching out to you directly in regard to this was a part of their requests. They wanted you to reach out to us when you were ready, and only when you were ready. We couldn't have foreseen it would have taken this long," he replied.

"Well, I guess they didn't either. It's just so hard to believe they didn't say anything about it at all. Like they were waiting for something specifically…"

THE DARK OF YOU KINDRA SOWDER

Like they were waiting for us to bond, Hyde interjected in my head.

The disturbing thought rolled through my mind like a tidal wave – nearly suffocating as I continued to follow at Mr. Segerson's back to the furthest wall in the room.

"I understand, Miss McAllister. Maybe," he said, turning toward me when he approached a blindingly red door, "they had their reasons. Or, it's as you've said, their passing was so sudden they ran out of time. I guess we will never know."

He grinned sadly, a surface type of grief moving into his expression.

"I guess not," mirroring the grin back at him.

The man before me didn't need to know I had been the one to end their lives ultimately. There was no reason to make sure he knew the complete story. Even after all this time, I still felt like I didn't understand everything that had taken place. Of course, only my parents did, and they were gone. Hyde has seen so much more and hid the information within herself to save me from too much trauma, but had let go of some tidbits over the last year.

131

Thankfully so.

With another swipe of his key card, the door slid open, revealing the largest room filled from ceiling to floor with silver safe deposit boxes embedded in white and gray granite.

"Wow," I breathed with a heavy sigh, eyes wide.

Without a single thought, I followed his steps into the massive room. The door slid closed behind me as soon as my feet crossed the threshold, only a soft hush of air at my back.

"It is rather impressive, isn't it?" he asked, only glancing back at me with a knowing grin.

"I think impressive is a bit of an understatement," I replied.

"I don't disagree," he said, looking away from me and moving toward the furthest wall and motioning with one hand toward it. "This is where we keep the safe deposit boxes of our VIP clients."

Out of nowhere, he produced a small silver key and inserted it into a seemingly random box at eye level. As soon as he turned it, I heard a lock inside the wall disengage, another door sliding open that was completely unnoticeable until that very moment. Then the room I recalled from the memory Hyde showed me came into view, and I followed Mr. Segerson blindly inside. This room didn't contain nearly as many safe deposit boxes as the larger one before it – maybe a quarter of what I estimated to be in the room we just left. There were a few small tables in the space, hinting at the fact the room was hardly used.

I stopped walking as I took it all in, my mind racing with the possibilities. Of course, I knew one thing my parents kept inside their own safe deposit box, but what were the stories of the others housed in that room? I wasn't certain I genuinely wanted to know. Our story was horrific enough as it was.

Mr. Segerson took a quick glance back at me before finally approaching a silver box housed to the right by one of the tables. He stood before the table, turned toward me, and folded his hands before placing them on the dark wooden surface. His face was stoic, nothing like I thought he would be. Expectant, maybe. But not stoic.

I took that as my cue.

Putting one foot in front of the other carefully, I approached the table and stood across from him – the same place my father and myself had stood in my memory.

"Are you ready, Miss McAllister?" he asked, the patient look on his face turning expectant with the words he spoke.

"As ready as I'll ever be," I said with a nod.

My heart pounded and my mind raced, Hyde remaining strangely quiet considering the circumstances. A part of me wanted to believe she wanted me to feel everything on my own without her interjecting, and another part of me felt something else was going on. What was she waiting for?

Mr. Segerson inserted the key into the box to remove it from the wall, handling it with absolute care as if there was a bomb inside. I knew that wouldn't have been the case. My parents sacrificed themselves to me so I could become what my biology had chosen. They were weird in that sense, but they weren't extremists. Blowing me up inside their bank with a man they trusted to keep this piece of our history – and whatever else lay inside – would not have been on their agenda.

Granted, there was nothing about any of this that was normal.

When he pulled the safe deposit box out of the wall and placed it on the table before me, my heart lurched in my chest. My entire body went stiff, frozen in place as he turned it so the next lock on the stop faced me. This lock was different. It required a fingerprint, which I wasn't certain they would have had. Hyde hadn't shown me as much, anyway.

I stared at the intimidating box until I heard Mr. Segerson clear his throat. My eyes shot up to his, meeting his concerned gaze.

"Miss McAllister, please place the index and middle fingers of your right hand on the scanner," he requested.

I couldn't move, and I couldn't look away from him. The request lingered in the air between us, abandoned to the quiet of the space. The only sound I could hear was my heart racing inside me, echoing in my ears past Hyde's deafening silence.

His eyes softened as he watched me, taking a deep breath before opening his mouth.

135

"I know this is hard," he started. "This is the last thing you have from your parents. I'm afraid that, aside from the funds in your account, this is the last they have left behind. Knowing this, I understand why you'd be fearful to uncover their last remaining earthbound secrets."

My mouth nearly dropped open at his words. He had pegged my feelings so well when I hadn't. Fear. I was terrified even though I knew what was inside. I didn't know what it meant, or exactly what it was, but I knew somehow.

Or was it Hyde who knew, and that was why she was so deathly quiet?

I pulled a deep breath in through my nose and decided that was the right moment to rip off the band-aid. It was now or never.

Without another moment's hesitation, I placed my fingers on the scanner. The lights to the side blinked red and then settled on green after a few intense seconds. A small beep sounded, and then the small sounds of locks disengaging broke the silence even further. The lid popped open slightly as my finger still rested on the scanner. Before I lost my nerve, I removed my hand and opened the lid all the way, laying its top edge against the table.

The velvet box that housed the necklace lay inside and, when I lifted the lid, Hyde's presence forced itself back into my head and body. As if she had been waiting like a coiled rattlesnake for the moment of revelation to come. My eyes burned with her unhinged rage and need as I removed the box from within, not touching the necklace just yet. If Hyde reacted this way just to its visible presence, I did not want to know what would happen if I touched it – especially not in a public setting in front of a practical stranger.

The green stone glowed slightly at my presence, an image of the statue in Adam's room barging into my memory. I nearly gasped as I stared down at it, recalling a vital piece of information. I didn't know what the statue was exactly, but I had a feeling I'd learn soon enough.

"Miss McAllister, will you be taking the items with you, or leaving them within our care?" Mr. Segerson asked barely audible in my current state.

"I will be taking them with me. Thank you. Please keep the box in my trust for future use if I see fit." I responded on autopilot. The gemstone was mesmerizing in its own rite which had my undivided attention currently.

"Very good, Miss McAllister. I will see you out when you are ready."

My eyes caught something still inside the safe deposit box – an envelope. Without putting the necklace down, I reached down and retrieved it with my free hand.

That was when I saw my name written in my mother's perfect penmanship on the thick cream paper.

They had written me a letter and I was certain every answer I was looking for would be there. I followed Mr. Segerson back through the labyrinth below the bank into the lobby where he bid me well and as I left through the large doors. I knew but one thing. Hyde has never had such a reaction to anything like she did to this necklace, and I did not know if I should be worried or not.

CHAPTER THIRTEEN

Our Dearest Daughter,

If you're reading this, we met our bloody demise as intended to solidify your bond with your innermost self. Your other self, as it was and is. With its intensity, the love of a parent can get in the way of such things. Every part of us wanted to see you grow into the amazing young woman we knew you would be, but we were on borrowed time as soon as you came into this world. The most horrible part of that was that we knew it all too well and would gladly give ourselves to you and for you, again.

Our bodies, minds, and souls were yours from the time you opened your eyes. Blythe, make no mistake, we knew exactly what we were doing by having you.

We're certain you've heard a lot of things about what lives inside you. At this point, we're also certain your bond with your other self has grown and forged so strongly that nothing could break it. Otherwise, you wouldn't have found this letter and what was enclosed inside the safe deposit box.

You were probably wondering why we didn't include this safe deposit box or its contents in the will presented to you upon our deaths. That, our dearest girl, was by design. We knew you would discover it just as I had when my time came. Your grandmother handed this down to me, and it has moved through our family through the ages. Quite honestly, longer than anyone ever thought to record in history.

It is your turn to keep our secrets, Blythe.

It has also been said that the stone within this necklace is the key to our origins. A link to the chain of our growing timeline. A piece of everyone before you is housed within, making it even more sacred. Guard it with your life. It may save you one day just as it had saved me.

As we write this letter to you, we can't help but imagine who you've become and how our loss has shaped you. Please don't blame yourself for what took place. We had every intention of following our plan through, even if it meant we lost you along the way. Just know this. We wouldn't have chosen anything else outside of our sacred duty. Our tradition. Our purpose

140

on this Earth once another generation came to being.
Every beat of our hearts belonged to you from the start.

Every beat.

As it was meant to be from the very beginning.

As it is meant to be for eternity. One day, perhaps it will come to be your destiny as well. That will be your ultimate decision.

With our undying love and devotion,

Mom & Dad

"Oh my God," was all I whispered as I held the letter in my lap, the box holding the necklace beside me on the couch.

Hyde didn't answer, letting me have my moment of peace to take in the last words of my parents. She wasn't completely silent. She still roared within me like a tidal wave begging to be set free once my eyes set upon the glowing green gem. Not much else had existed for her since, but somehow, she let me have this. Like it was just as important to her as it was to me.

THE DARK OF YOU Kindra Sowder

I would have said that meant the world to me if she didn't always have ulterior motives.

Even after all I had seen, all that I had done, nothing had prepared me for this. Not even the dreams I had about my parents in a drug-induced state thanks to Adam's lackeys.

Not even after hearing their words in my head after that was I prepared for this. A piece of the puzzle of who I was lay beside me, beckoning to me and the monster within like a beacon of sheer horror. My body wouldn't stop humming with the energy emitting from it. It was as if every nerve ending was on fire, tingling with flames that didn't burn – but revived. Strengthened from the very core of what made me what I was and solidified my bond with Hyde even further than my parents death.

I felt horrified, grief-stricken all over again, and powerful. It was a terrifying, heady mixture of emotions that eclipsed the fear I felt once Adam had revealed himself to us. And I couldn't stop it.

Now every single emotion mixed in a swirling whirlpool of power and chaos.

THE DARK OF YOU   KINDRA SOWDER

We've been waiting for this for a long time,
Hyde whispered in my mind.

"Then why did you feel the need to repress the
memory at all? Why not help me find this earlier?" I
asked to the empty air. I stood and approached the only
mirror in the living room, glaring at my reflection.
"Why wait?"

The expression on my face changed in the
reflection from one of anger and resentment to one of
knowing and rage. It twisted my features, so I almost
didn't recognize myself, my eyes also turning the same
bright green of the gemstone within the closed velvet
box behind me.

It wasn't the right time, Blythe, she replied, a
near hiss to our shared voice.

"It's never the right time," was all I knew to say
before I turned away from the mirror and stared down
at the box on the couch.

What could I do with it? It wasn't something I
could just put on and wear on a night out. It was a
treasure – a dangerous treasure if Hyde's reaction to it
was any indication of its purpose. My parents said it
was my turn to keep our family's secrets, but there was

so much of the puzzle still missing. Every part of me screamed with unreleased tension.

I rolled my neck, every vertebra cracking in response.

There was one thing I knew for certain. The gem housed within that box was linked to Hyde, Adam, and that statue in Adam's kill room. I racked my brain, trying to figure out exactly how it all fit together, but couldn't figure it out just yet. And Hyde had said it wasn't the right time before now to expose this partial truth to me. Now it was my turn to figure out the rest, but I would have to have Hyde's help. There was no way around that. She would have to give me something more than this.

"That's where I'll keep it," I said, coming to a quick decision before my mind could fully register it.

I barely took the time to think about it as I grabbed the box, ran into my bedroom, and opened the hidden door to my kill room. No one would look there. As far as I was aware, Hyde had never taken Adam there, which meant me and Hyde were the only living beings that knew about it at all. I had never shown it to Emmett, which made it perfect.

THE DARK OF YOU   Kindra Sowder

My feet crossed the threshold before I could stop myself. The room was immaculately cleaned after Hyde's last kill inside it, everything bleached, and all evidence of our crimes destroyed. Outside of this room, I still had no clue what Hyde did to conceal the physical evidence she thankfully never allowed me to assist with. She did it all on her own, and maybe that was a blessing in disguise. That way, if I ever caved to the detective, I wouldn't know where the bodies were buried.

Literally.

I opened the cabinet in the room that housed all the tools of the trade and gently placed the box among the wide array of saws, screwdrivers, and other utensils used for torture. This was the perfect place to keep secrets, and I couldn't think of a better spot. No one would look for it – if anyone else even knew it existed. I had a strong feeling that no one did. Especially, if my family was able to keep it hidden so well and for so long.

As if the universe thought it was a wonderful time for my homicidal secrets to be laid bare to the world, I heard the door to my apartment open and the jingling of keys echo down the hall.

THE DARK OF YOU KINDRA SOWDER

"Honey, I'm home," Lauren said as I heard the door close behind her along with a shuffle of a paper bag.

My eyes shot to the open door to my kill room, my heart lurching in my chest as soon as her voice boomed through the apartment. My instincts for self-preservation kicked in instantly. I closed the cabinet, eyes barely glancing over the incriminating things housed inside. Before I knew it, my feet carried me to the door, and I closed it as quickly and quietly as I could so as not to alert Lauren of the room's existence. Then I raced out of my bedroom and down the hall, coming into the living room as she placed the large brown bag on the couch.

"Hey," I said through the intake of a deep breath. "What are you doing here? Did we have plans, and I forgot?"

She smiled and put her purse down beside the bag, crossing her arms over her chest and turning to me. Her eyes met mine and I saw something within them. That knowing surfaced, but she would never mention I'd been acting suspiciously. I mean, I had been lately. Even I could see that.

THE DARK OF YOU KINDRA SOWDER

Ever since Adam revealed himself. Now even more secrets laid themselves bare for me. Secrets I knew I could never share. Even with my best friend.

"Nope. With the cops sniffing around I figured you could use a night in. Not like we do that very often," she explained. "I have ice cream, bad Chinese food, and booze. I even got all the right stuff to make that Old-Fashioned thingy you love so much. So, where do you want to start?"

"You don't want to go out and make extremely bad decisions?" I asked, brow furrowing.

I couldn't say I wasn't grateful for her presence. If she hadn't shown up, I wasn't sure what would have happened. Would I have snapped? Or Hyde? Hyde had been practically purring over the necklace as soon as I opened the safe deposit box. And that reaction made me more nervous than if Lauren had gotten past my awareness and into the kill room when I had the door wide open. As if I wanted to get caught.

"If you ask my parents, hanging out with you anywhere is an unwise decision. We can plop down on the couch, stuff ourselves, get drunk, and fall asleep. The hangover alone would make up for us not going out, and there's no risk of date rape," she said.

"You make so much sense right now, it's scary," I replied.

"So," she started, taking out a bottle of tequila, a bag full of the ingredients for my drink of choice, a bottle of Dewars, and a carton of what smelled to be lo Mein and holding them up, "where do you want to start? Expensive booze, bad food, or bad booze?"

I looked over my options and grinned back at her.

"Why not all the above?" I said with a shrug.

She squealed, put the goodies back inside the bags, picked them up, and made her way to the kitchen. As I watched her walk away one thought caused my stomach to turn.

Good thing my freezer was empty.

CHAPTER FOURTEEN

"Blythe," a shrill voice screamed, jarring me from darkness.

I couldn't place the screams as the cloud of fatigue lifted and my awareness came back slowly – crawled like an infant just rising to its hands and knees for the first time.

"Blythe," the voice shrieked again. "Blythe, wake up! Can you hear me?"

Anguish filled those cries. Anguish and something else I couldn't quite place. I felt it in my core and my heart, Hyde's presence rising to the surface along with me as everything returned to focus. Then it hit me.

The voice.

The screams were Lauren's, and I struggled to pull myself out of the void as my heart lurched in my chest. What had we been doing before we fell asleep? We had been laughing, watching an awful B-rated horror movie while drinking and eating the cheap

Chinese food she brought over. It was a welcome night with just the two of us where the stress and pressure of it all seemed to melt away.

Where were we now? Fear took residence in my chest, surrounding my heart and gripping it so tight my chest filled with pain.

"Blythe," she screamed again.

It was that moment I placed the other emotion I heard in her voice. Terror. Horror beyond anything she had ever seen.

My eyes snapped open, and I gasped. My vision a complete blur of images and crimson. Blood. I pulled in another ragged breath, the pain in my chest easing just enough. Blinking past the blurriness, the color of crimson shifted across my eyes. Where it moved, there was a heaviness there. I blinked again, Lauren's cries at my back causing my heart to break. Pain flooded my body as I lay on my side on a concrete floor. The blurred images of where I was made it impossible to know where we had ended up.

"Blythe. Oh my, God," Lauren gasped, placing her hands gingerly on my side.

THE DARK OF YOU Kindra Sowder

Her touch sent fire rippling through me, but I didn't push her away. Her touch helped me feel grounded in some way, the pain I woke up in fading almost as if it had never existed. It nipped at the very edges of my awareness like a pack of wolves.

You're welcome, I heard Hyde say in my mind.

I couldn't stop the groan that left my lips as I closed my eyes, thankful that it wasn't too bright in the room I could barely make out. The concrete floor beneath me told me we may have been in a warehouse, but I wasn't sure. Opening my eyes again, the world became much clearer, the blood in my eyes nearly gone as my eyes watered uncontrollably.

I recognized the place instantly and jerked myself upright. I heard Lauren squeal as if I had nearly pushed her over, but I didn't care. My eyes darted around, unable to find a threat.

The place I woke up in was the place I had lived a nightmare – one that Hyde helped cushion the blow of so I could be with Emmett without what they did to me hanging over my head.

This was the place I had been tortured, raped, and found out the true depths of who I was.

THE DARK OF YOU   KINDRA SOWDER

This was Hell.

"What the fuck happened?" I asked, my voice a lot meaner than I intended.

I turned slowly to face Lauren, every muscle in my body almost screaming as the pain and tension faded. My heart raced, the dregs of adrenaline wearing off from what I assumed was some altercation. Then, what I saw as I finally faced her and took in the scene behind her solidified my assumption. Fresh crimson covered the concrete floor, mixing with the old that was left behind from Johan and Mitch's demise. Hyde had eaten their hearts, not leaving them to waste, so I knew the brain matter I saw on the far wall had been the result of whatever happened.

"You don't remember?" Lauren asked, worry etched on her face.

I shook my head, staring at the brain matter and blood plastered all over the far wall, her wide-eyed expression in my periphery. Hyde stirred slightly, and I knew this had to have something to do with her. And now the possibility of Lauren knowing my deepest, darkest secret loomed. I wanted to scream, cry, and curse the monster inside me for their lack of impulse control in some of the most important moments.

152

THE DARK OF YOU KINDRA SOWDER

Lauren's presence was not the right time to do whatever she had done. Never.

A loud metal screech sounded from behind me and my head jerked around toward the source. Jackson's lumbering form clad in all black stepped in, closing the door loudly behind him. He rubbed his hands together as if they were cold, his eyes meeting mine almost instantly. His were resolute while mine burned with unshed tears.

"We have quite a mess on our hands, Blythe," he said, voice calm and reassuring.

"What did she do?" I asked, almost silently.

Jackson didn't want to look at me as soon as I asked, his eyes avoiding meeting my face. They bounced around the room, settling on a place behind my head. Glancing back at Lauren, I saw the fear there. She had seen something, and we weren't dealing with any messes until I knew what. I had kept her away from all this until now. I needed to know what caused my plan to keep her as far away from the blood as possible to crumble.

"Jackson, please," I said, looking back at him. "What did *she* do?"

THE DARK OF YOU   KINDRA SOWDER

"I didn't do anything. I swear," Lauren said behind me.

I felt a tinge of guilt, cringing at her words knowing she hadn't done anything, but felt I was accusing her.

Of course, there wasn't an easy answer to any of this that I could provide her.

It was that moment I realized how badly my head ached through the haze, Lauren and Jackson distracting me from what I felt. The blood in my vision had mostly cleared, but now a part of my scalp stung right at my hairline. I reached up, touching it gingerly. It stung even more at the contact and, when I pulled my hand away, blood coated my fingertips. As I sat there and stared at the bright red that began to drip down toward my palm, I thought about how to explain any of this to my best friend.

CHAPTER FIFTEEN

After a few silent moments, Jackson watching me carefully as I weighed my options, he said he would clean everything up and we should head home. I didn't have to be told twice.

"I'll come to your apartment in an hour after this is dealt with to stitch that up," he said as he pointed to my sliced forehead.

All I could do was nod. Lauren and I walked to her waiting car – which she hardly ever drove – and then quietly drove to my apartment. The entire ride up the elevator was much the same. Once we walked into my apartment and Lauren sat down, I opened my mouth to speak and explain. It would be a long night of questions, but I was prepared for that. I just never thought it would come to this.

"Wait," she said, holding her hand up to silence me, "I need another minute."

Her mascara ran down her face as if she had been crying the entire way home. It was then I decided I was a horrible friend. I hadn't looked at her once since

155

we entered the apartment building, avoiding her gaze at all costs.

Avoiding her inevitable judgment.

Her body trembled, her fingers shaking as she wrung her hands in her lap. All I could do was observe, remaining silent as she seemingly processed everything she probably saw. I felt ashamed that I couldn't remember any of what took place, but I was fairly certain Hyde would be filling in the blanks sometime soon. Not remembering didn't stop the guilt I felt. It moved through my mind and body like a living being – a virus – taking over every part of my body.

Hyde was a parasite, and now she managed to take the one thing I had succeeded in keeping out of her grasp for years.

The time clicked on and on, the only sounds were the hush of the air conditioning and the ticking clock above my fireplace. It had only been a few minutes before she looked me in the eye and opened her mouth to speak, but it felt like hours.

"You were… different," she stated.

"Yes, I–" I started.

THE DARK OF YOU   Kindra Sowder

She held her hand up again, stopping me as her eyes bore into mine.

"You were different. Your eyes were different," she continued. "You… you left the apartment, so I followed you. I shouldn't have followed you. But you… you lured this guy to that warehouse. I followed you in." She paused for a moment, seeming to process what she would say next. "You were hurting him. I came in and distracted you, and he hit you with something. It all happened so fast. Jackson came in and shot him in the head. I don't even know how Jackson knew where we were, but he did. And he shot the man. He killed him. Oh, my God."

I saw her crumbling before me. I knelt in front of her, taking her hands in mine.

"I know. I'm sorry. You shouldn't have had to see any of this. I am so, so sorry," I said. "I've tried to keep you away from this since we met."

She didn't respond for a second, her eyes searching mine as they brimmed with tears.

"We've been friends since college," she sniffed.

"Yeah," I said with a nod.

"You've been…" she stopped like she couldn't say the word, "for that long?"

"Longer," I said. "Since high school. Since before my parents died."

"How?" she asked.

She didn't have to say more. I knew what she was asking. I rose from my knees and sat beside her, her eyes following me the entire time as if I would strike at any moment. I had no intention of hurting her. Even Hyde remained silent, so I had a feeling she wouldn't be either.

"It's a long story," I stated.

"Then we'll be up all goddamned night. I want an explanation for what I saw," she answered. "Not like we don't have sick days at work. Hannah can deal without us for a day."

"You sure you want to know?" I asked, eyebrows furrowing with genuine concern.

She adjusted on the couch, facing me.

"Brew some coffee. I'll be right here," she practically ordered.

"You sure you don't want wine? Or liquor?"

She grinned slightly, but it didn't reach her eyes.

"We'll see how it goes, I guess," she said. "You can start while we wait."

I did as requested, quickly brewing the strongest pot of coffee I had in my entire existence. While we waited, I sat next to her on the couch, taking the place I had been sitting before the shit literally hit the fan.

I wasn't certain what I should include – whether she needed to know about Emmett and Adam or not. So, I began with my own family. Then I'd follow up with the documents in my room. If she had more questions, I'd answer them the best I could. The books and the documents could fill in so many rabbit holes I hadn't even looked down yet. It was just too much all at once.

"I was different tonight," I started. "What you saw was part of what you could call a family curse. I have a part of me…" I paused to think of my next words carefully, "kind of like another person…"

"Multiple personalities?" she asked, worry crossing her features.

"In a way, I guess you could say," I replied. "Except this is actually *another* entity inside me. It really exists. It's not just a part of my mind that got blocked off. It's me. But not me. I don't know if it's making any sense at all. I've never had to explain it."

Lauren nodded, her eyes moving off to the side as if she were thinking.

"Kind of like the Hulk?" she cracked with a smile, gaze meeting mine again.

"Ummm, I guess you could say that. Except she comes whenever she wants…"

"And only your eyes turn green," Lauren stated, her smile dropping. "But you were scary."

"I know. I'm sorry."

"Can you control it?" she asked. "What does it make you do?"

"*She* is crazy. Homicidal," I stated. "Damn near psychotic."

"You've killed people. Is that what you were going to do to that man?" Lauren asked, her brow furrowing as she watched my every move carefully.

Like a rattlesnake ready to strike.

Hyde hummed within me in response, answering her question without words. Of course, she was. She had been ramped up by the presence of the necklace my parents left me. That much was clear when she responded so violently inside me. I should have known she would go this far, but I didn't think she would be stupid enough to do it with someone else in the apartment. Our presence at that warehouse was easily explained by Lauren's presence. If she hadn't been there, Hyde would have led the poor unsuspecting man to my apartment and our kill room.

"That's what *she* was going to do, yes," I responded.

"How many?"

"Too many. Far too many to count."

"What does she do with them when she's done?"

"I don't know." I shook my head. "Everything goes dark when she's done."

I watched her focus shift to a spot on her jeans – a spot I assumed was blood. I still didn't remember what had happened. Hyde hadn't shown it to me yet, and I didn't feel like asking Lauren for more details was the best idea. With an inward sigh, I adjusted on the couch and observed her for a moment. She seemed okay, but Lauren had ways of masking her true thoughts at the worst of times. I knew she wasn't all right, but she wasn't going to tell me. Not right now.

She wanted to know everything and, since I was still hard at work learning myself, I could only think of what I could offer her other than my words and half-baked explanations.

"Hey," I said to pull her attention. I reached out and tapped her knee with my index finger. "You want a cup of coffee or a glass of wine?"

"Coffee sounds good."

"Great," I exclaimed, rising from the couch. "Since I'm still learning about this myself, and all of this is so hard to explain, I actually have a box of documents and old journals that may help us both understand this a little better. What do you say we go read?"

I knew more than I let on. More than I could willingly tell her that wouldn't make me look like just a monster. There was no way conceivable I could let her see me that way. She probably did already, but it felt like this was a secret I needed for myself.

THE DARK OF YOU KINDRA SOWDER

My biggest secret had been divulged unwillingly to my best friend. If there was anything I could, and would, keep to myself, I would. I couldn't let her know that I was a monster too. That was the role Hyde would happily play for me.

THE DARK OF YOU KINDRA SOWDER

CHAPTER SIXTEEN

It hadn't even been an hour and Lauren had read through a decent amount of the journal Adam gifted me. She stood after reading about my ancestor in Salem and paced while biting her fingernails. There was a distinct *click* as her teeth broke small pieces of her nails with each step she took across my marbled floors. Her section hadn't been far into the journal, but there was plenty at the beginning I had passed over, Hyde bringing me to that section before I had a chance to delve into it myself.

I had learned a lot in those sections as we looked through it, but hers still stuck out in my mind up to that point. There were tidbits about others, but another had caught my attention. One alive at the time of Christ who had even watched his crucifixion. I could admit this condition could turn even the most devout Christian into an atheist. I still didn't believe but being armed with the knowledge he walked the Earth as a human being and someone like me walked it with him – I almost couldn't fathom it.

THE DARK OF YOU   KINDRA SOWDER

Even Lauren's eyebrows had raised with surprise as we read the words, both sitting on the floor with mugs of steaming coffee between us.

After a few heartbeats, the door to my apartment opened I heard the unmistakable footfalls of Jackon's heavy boots echo through the empty air. A few seconds later he loomed in the doorway of my bedroom, eyes widening at the sight of the journal and the box containing the rest of the documents provided to me.

"You look like you've seen a ghost, Jackson," I said, rising from my position on the floor with a mug in hand.

"I don't think this is what he had in mind when he gave these to you," he replied in a most serious tone of baritone, hands motioning toward the journal and box.

"Well, I never had Lauren learning about any of this in mind either, but my best laid plans fucking changed. Hyde saw to that," I said.

"Fair enough," Jackson said, watching Lauren as she continued to pace. "Are you ready for me to stitch that up?"

THE DARK OF YOU   KINDRA SOWDER

He pointed to my forehead. That was the first time I noticed the first aid kit in his hand other hand at his side. I had a feeling the split in my forehead had most likely healed somewhat as Lauren and I delved into the madness that was Adam, Hyde, and the others, but I'd let him look regardless.

"Sure," I said, sitting down on the bed. "We'll do this in here."

"Okay," he said with a nod.

He entered the room, placing the kit on the bed as he approached and stood before me. With swift, quiet movements, he removed an alcohol swab and began to wipe the blood from my forehead. I could have showered, but time was of the essence in this situation. Plus, this was more important. Learning more about myself alongside my unsuspecting friend was more important than removing the sweat and blood that remained from Hyde's excursion and near miss.

"That man could have killed you, Blythe. What were you thinking?" he asked as he continued to wipe away the copious amounts of dried and congealed blood from out of my hairline.

"You want to tell Hyde that?" I asked. "It was all her. I don't even remember what the hell happened."

"And you have explained all that to your friend?"

"I probably know more than I should, at this point," Lauren said. "Don't act like I'm not here."

"You *shouldn't* be here," Jackson pointedly remarked with an accusatory tone.

The alcohol wipe connected with raw flesh, making me hiss. I jerked back slightly, anger unfurling in my chest at the burn as well as the tone he took with Lauren.

"You can't say you wouldn't have followed her if she just left without a word, Mr. Clean," Lauren snapped.

"That's enough," I said, tone stern enough to draw their respective attentions. "The fact is that we're all here. We all know. And we all must deal with this... now. It's a mess, but this is where we're at. Hyde put us in this position because she couldn't control herself. Fuck. No surprises there actually. *That* shouldn't have happened. Period."

THE DARK OF YOU KINDRA SOWDER

As soon as the words left my mouth, I felt the telltale signs of Hyde's presence within. Her growl rumbled deep in my chest, almost an audible snarl that I swallowed to suppress. She was angry with me, but from what little I knew, she almost blew our cover completely. Not that there was much of a cover to begin with. She's simply good at covering her tracks.

"I'm going to have to tell Adam. You know that," Jackson nearly spat as he turned back to me and touched the wound with alcohol.

"No one is telling him," I ordered.

"Wait," Lauren said, stopping dead in her tracks. "Adam? The first? From your journal?"

When I looked at her, I saw the terror in her eyes. It twinkled in her brown eyes, nearly erupting into the fire of fear.

"The one and only," Jackson answered.

"Shit," she whispered.

"Shit is right," I answered. "That's why no one is saying a word. Hyde already put her at risk, Jackson. I can't have her and Adam posing an even greater threat."

THE DARK OF YOU   Kindra Sowder

"Blythe…" Jackson started, shaking his head.

"Jackson. I can't lose my best friend. Either you let me have this, or you have blood on your hands. He does not like secrets. He kept a major one from me for months, so I would be right to keep my only ally a damn secret."

"She's not your only ally," he scoffed.

"You work for him," I laughed. "You're *his* ally. Not mine. Adam is not to find out. Understand me?"

"Sure thing," Jackson said glaring at my forehead. "Looks like you've already healed up enough I don't need to stitch you up. Just keep it clean."

"Sure. Yeah," I replied.

Spotting Lauren behind Jackson, her eyes were wide as she stared at his broad back – face pale. Recognition lit up her brown eyes, and her mouth slacked open. Her hand raised and she pointed at him. Her eyes shifted back and forth between the two of us.

"You're…" she stammered. "I've seen you with Emmett. I knew I recognized you, but I didn't want to say anything in case I was wrong but…"

Jackson turned to look at her, hands dropping the supplies into the first aid kit. His brow furrowed with frustration, and he opened his mouth to speak.

"Lauren, I–" I interrupted.

"I've seen you all together. You, Emmett, and that woman with the… hair. What's her name? Cyra," Lauren muttered, eyes growing with shock with each word.

She looked as if she knew something she shouldn't, other than what she had seen. She knew. I felt it deep in my bones, and Hyde unfurled within me even more as if she needed to act. I swallowed her down, pushing her so far down she couldn't resurface unless I allowed her to.

"Get your dog, Blythe. Before I have to," Jackson warned, jaw clenched hard.

"I am not someone's dog, asshole," Lauren shouted. "But you are, and I know exactly who he is now. He's a monster. I should have recognized him from that book, but somehow I didn't. Now, I know."

Jackson's eyebrows raised a fraction, and he turned to me with a knowing smirk.

"He's not the only one," Jackson stated. "Your friend here is quite the monster herself, but I try not to judge. Considering…"

"I sat here with Blythe all night and read that journal. I'm not an idiot. I know what she's done, but that journal gave me enough information to know he is much worse than she is. At least hers tries to save her from what it's done," Lauren explained. "Your boss has carved one hell of a bloody path through history. That's pretty damn obvious. You don't live that long without doing so."

"She's smarter than I gave her credit for," he muttered, closing the first aid kit with a soft click.

"You don't give many people credit, if we're being honest here," I said.

"True," he replied. "Then maybe you should show her your *room*. Maybe then she'll understand your monster a little bit better."

"What… room?" she asked.

I glared at him, willing holes to appear in his face. I hadn't planned to show her anything more for a while. She needed space to digest what she just learned

– not more shoved down her throat when she was at capacity.

"Transparency, Blythe," was all he said before he picked up the kit and sauntered out of my bedroom.

I froze in place as she stared at me, listening to his footsteps and then the door of my apartment thudding shut. I couldn't move. I couldn't breathe. All I could do was watch her as I saw hurt develop in her eyes that even though I was being more honest with her than I had ever been, I was still withholding. Without another word, I stood and walked to the part of the wall that housed the hidden door that led to Hyde's room of pain.

Reaching out, I brushed my fingers over the small button, the hidden door sliding open silently – Hyde's torture chamber revealed. There was nowhere else to hide.

"What the hell is that?" Lauren asked.

"Hyde's favorite place on Earth," I replied with a weary sigh.

Lauren took a painstakingly slow step forward, stopping short. Craning her neck, her eyes moved from object to object. Her expression went from curious to angry and revolted within a few seconds, and I knew letting her see it was a mistake. But I couldn't have hidden it for long. So, in the interest of transparency that Lauren had well earned, I had to rip off that band-aid. Harshly.

She opened her mouth as if to say something, snapping it shut quickly before any words came out. Then her mouth opened again, a pitiful croak coming from her throat. When she glanced at me, she quickly looked away and took a step backward.

Before I could think of anything to say to make this better, she turned on her heel and ran – the only sound of her exit was the slam of the door.

CHAPTER SEVENTEEN

I had considered chasing after Lauren when she took off but quickly decided she needed space. And time. Something I could afford to give her. There was no fear of her going to the police to report me – or Emmett. She was far too intelligent to make that type of egregious mistake, and it wasn't because of me. Adam had made it this far without ever being caught through the centuries. The journal had told us that much.

No one would be catching him now. Not for any reason.

His ability to remain hidden all that time while killing unceremoniously was rather impressive. Hyde had carved her own bloody path, but she was careful unlike so many before.

Once my mind settled, I ran a scalding bath that would melt the flesh off anyone else. I wasn't as filthy as I imagined I would be, the blood only centrally located on my head where I had been injured. The memory of what took place in the warehouse – or even before that – still had not surfaced as I lowered myself into the steaming water.

The sigh left my lips without my permission as I sank into it, every part of my body singing with heat. It felt cleansing as if it could wash the last twenty-four hours away.

Hyde moved through my body as well, threatening to take over every corner and every cell – wanting to make every fold and crevice of my mind hers. Taking a deep breath, I sunk down into the water, submerging completely. The blood from my forehead rippled away from me and through the water, turning it a deep crimson tinged with brown.

You can't drown me out, Hyde hummed in my head. *Hell Blythe, you can't even drown me.*

I squeezed my eyes shut, listening to the barely audible yet muffled noises of city life on the streets below passing through the water surrounding me. Hyde risked our lives for a kill, and I couldn't forgive her for that. Not that she was asking for my forgiveness. She never did, nor would she ever. She didn't require it from anyone, for any reason. But we were partners in this life. It was something we had agreed to, and she was quick to break that trust.

THE DARK OF YOU KINDRA SOWDER

My lungs began to burn with the need for oxygen, and it would be so easy to stay here – let the water fill my lungs and end it all. If Hyde would let me. If Hyde would allow this sick, twisted game to be over.

A new sound made its way into my warm cocoon. Footsteps followed by the muffled sound of someone saying my name. A female voice. My eyes shot open, and a figure stood over me. Bright pink hair the color of cotton candy stood out along with black sheathing her body, and I couldn't hold my breath any longer. I shot up with a gasp, not even trying to hide my surprise. Water poured over my face, but I didn't wipe it away. I stared at her through the sting of hot water, my heart threatening to break past its prison of bone.

"Cyra," I panted. "What the fuck?"

"Don't be a prude, Blythe. When you've seen one pair of tits and a vag, you've seen them all," Cyra stated, rolling her eyes.

"That's not the issue," I stated, pushing my wet hair away from my face. "You broke into my home. If you're here to kill me, get it over with. I have shit to take care of, and none of it includes you."

"You're right," she said as she sat very casually on the edge of the tub.

"I know I'm right…" I started.

"Not for the reason you think," she said.

"You have no idea what I'm thinking."

"That may be the case, but something came to me in a vision."

"Like I said before, stop with that bullshit," I said with a frustrated growl. "That ruse is getting old. You showed your true colors. Just stop."

Her face shifted, nonchalance turning into the same ruthless contempt I felt in return.

"Fine. I was sent here with a message for you," she answered.

Irritation bloomed in my chest, and Hyde reacted unfavorably to her presence as well. At least there was one thing we could agree on. My jaw clenched, the muscles working as I used all my effort not to grab her by the back of the neck and drown her right there in the bathtub.

"And that message is?" I asked, making sure she heard my annoyance.

THE DARK OF YOU   KINDRA SOWDER

"It's from Emmett," she said bluntly. "Well, Adam." She tilted her head to the side. "Actually, I'm not one hundred percent certain who the request came from. It's so hard to tell sometimes."

"The difference is all in the eyes, Cyra. Unless you're blind," I stated.

She looked perturbed at that moment as if I struck a nerve. Her eyes darted to me and away toward the mirror across the bathroom and her body language shifted. She crossed her arms over her chest and crossed her legs as she sat beside me, refusing to look at me again – that cool confidence she had very recently leeching away.

Her armor had fallen briefly, and I couldn't stop myself from chipping away at it a little more. Hyde purred inside me, enjoying her unease as well.

"He hasn't shown himself to you," I said.

It wasn't a question. Her change in demeanor told me everything I needed to know. Then it made me wonder. *Why hadn't he? Did he not wholly trust her? Or was it something else? And why did Cyra take it so personally? Why did it hurt her?*

She didn't respond, only continued to look in the mirror like her reflection would give her the courage to respond. She wasn't like me or Emmett, so I knew that couldn't be the case. There was always a way to tell when someone near me was like me. Even though I didn't really know it, Hyde sensed it and quieted in Emmett's presence. It had alerted me to the fact that he was different, but I would have never guessed he was just like me. In any way. I had never met one aside from my parents growing up, so I figured we were such a rarity that I never would.

And here Cyra was, seemingly wanting to desperately be a part of what we were. In a way, I couldn't fault her for that, but even I wouldn't want this looking in from the outside.

Finally, she shook it off, looked at me, and locked eyes.

"I've seen him," she said, eyes shifting to the left instead of continuing to meet my gaze.

Lie. Even Hyde felt the lie lingering between us.

"It wasn't a question," I said, but didn't press it. How uncomfortable she looked said enough. "What's the message, Cyra?"

180

"He wants you to meet him at his apartment," she replied. "He also told me to tell you to wear something... black tie."

"Black tie?" I asked. "For what?"

"You'll just have to see," she said, standing up with a sigh.

"You don't know," I said – again, not a question.

She didn't respond again, just stood over me with her arms crossed and eyes blazing with anger. Obviously, it didn't take much to set her off. Or Emmett and Adam were a sore spot for her. Either way, I couldn't let her get the same reaction out of me. I had to remain calm while still letting her know I was someone for her to fear.

I decided our discussion was over, letting out the water so the blood, sweat, and fear from the most recent events washed down the drain along with my secrets. Standing, the water dripped down my body. Cyra's eyes flicked over me like she was appraising me. Trying to see what Emmett and Adam saw in me – why they chose me. I hated to tell her it was a multitude of reasons, the thing writhing inside me being a major player in the game Adam played. For Adam, a part of it had to do specifically with me, but Hyde was his true obsession. Our bond was something he marveled at. He just happened to also worship the body that housed it.

I stepped out and reached for my towel, covering myself for her benefit as goosebumps erupted over my flesh. Rolling my neck, a few vertebrae cracked. The stress from the last twenty-four hours had every muscle in my neck and shoulders in knots. The hot water had done little to melt them away, but at least the blood was gone. Of course, any stress relief the bath would have given me was instantly replaced by Cyra's mere presence.

"I guess I'll figure something out. Not like I don't have an entire closet to choose from," I said, moving past her and into my bedroom.

Her shoulder grazed mine as I passed her, and I heard her anger come out in a quiet huff of air from her lungs. That sigh alone let me know I had won this small showdown if that was what it was. Everything with her seemed to be since Adam had revealed himself. She didn't have to hide herself or her true intentions anymore.

THE DARK OF YOU   Kindra Sowder

"He's expecting you this evening," she said as she followed me out of the bathroom, her shoes clacking on the tiling.

I turned to her and looked over my shoulder with a wide smile, taking my time as I walked away from her and toward the closet doors. She avoided the trail of watery footprints I left in my wake, watching me as if to gauge my reaction to the order. I didn't see it as such. Whenever Adam surfaced, it was always at night.

"Then I've got plenty of time. When will Jackson be arriving to pick me up?" I asked.

"Around seven," she said.

I opened the bright white closet doors, exposing the racks of clothing, shoes, and jewelry within. There was far too much to choose from, but it wasn't all that was requested. Not even a quarter of it was. Most of my attire I could wear to the gallery or an exhibition. Or a date.

As I strode inside, I didn't respond. I didn't feel like a reply was necessary. What could I say that wasn't gloating of some sort?

"I saw the blood in the water, Blythe," she said. "I'd hate for him to find out."

"Find out what, Cyra?" I asked, turning toward her. "Is that a threat?" Hyde's gravelly tone surfaced in my voice.

Blinding heat ran through my veins and concentrated in my eyes, the change in my body obvious as Hyde came forward to terrify the woman before us.

Cyra's eyes went wide for a second before she regained her composure, every muscle in her body tense as she watched the shift in my eyes and posture. She didn't know anything. We both knew that, but it didn't stop the rage that enveloped us.

It didn't stop the hate.

She didn't know anything, but there was no way of knowing what she would say. It could be something detrimental, and we couldn't have that.

"Get out," I hissed, letting Hyde's presence strengthen.

THE DARK OF YOU   Kindra Sowder

It didn't take long – only a second – before she turned and nearly sprinted out of the apartment. Just like Lauren not long before.

THE DARK OF YOU KINDRA SOWDER

CHAPTER EIGHTEEN

Hyde sang within me as I admired my form in the long, mossy green silk gown. The heart-shaped neckline accentuated my cleavage, dipping down past my breastbone – no sleeves, no straps. Its silken lengths met the floor, silver-studded stilettos keeping it from dragging.

Black tie, as requested. The question as to why it mattered lingered for a moment, but it didn't bother me. I'd do anything he asked of me.

It had only been a few minutes with her at the forefront of my consciousness before the box with the necklace was in our shared hands, quickly adorned around my neck. The gem rested perfectly between my breasts, gleaming in the artificial light the kill room offered.

Jackson picked me up as usual and silently drove to Adam's apartment. No more pretenses. No more lies. Which meant Emmett's apartment was hardly a place we visited anymore. I had meant to ask him about it at one point, but so much had happened since it didn't seem that important.

Why it had popped into my head on the drive was beyond me. Maybe my mind needed to fill the silence besides the constant hum of Hyde's homicidal energy. It moved through my mind and my entire body, settling in the place between my legs as if Adam/Emmett were already nearby.

In twenty minutes, I stood in the empty living room of the lavish apartment. My home was modern sleek lines, but Adam had even more contemporary taste. Clean white walls stood bare, not even a single painting in sight. Then I felt it.

The pull of his presence in my mind, body, heart, and soul. I felt it so deeply I couldn't ignore it.

My entire body began to hum softly just under my skin as his footfalls sounded behind me. The footsteps were soft, and purposeful, almost as if he glided across the floor. It was at that instant I knew exactly who approached.

Emmett was in control.

I nearly sighed with relief but knew it wouldn't remain that way for much longer. I had to soak up every moment we had together before both our monsters took over. If I had a way to force them back into the darkness where they came from, never to surface again, I would have done anything. Even sold my soul, if that was what it took.

Emmett's finger lightly traced the portion of my back the gown left exposed. Another sigh left my lips without my permission, his touch tingling through every cell of my body. Hyde responded, knowing Adam was just within reach. She couldn't have him yet. This was the time she had promised me when we made the pact at my most vulnerable. She owed me this.

She lurched in my chest again, and I sneered, a growl almost escaping my throat in protest. I swallowed it down and pushed her back where she belonged as far as I could.

Don't. It's not your turn. Not yet, I thought, communicating with her without speaking a word.

His fingertip never left my skin, tracing along my spine in chill-inducing curves. I shivered in response. He moved closer, moving his hand down my arm to take my hand in his as his chest pressed against my back. My fingers automatically laced through his, closing with an unspoken promise. He leaned closer, his warmth enveloping me. His lips grazed the curve of my neck, chills of unmet need erupting over my entire body.

"Hello, beautiful," he whispered, lips grazing my ear lobe.

"Hi," I replied with a small grin.

"How did you find something like this so fast? You look... ravishing," he said, the most minute hint of a growl from Adam seeping through.

"I just happened to have this in the back of my closet," I answered as Hyde responded inside my body to Adam's emerging presence. "What's the occasion?"

I turned to Emmett, needing to see his burning browns before they changed into the sinister blue of Adam's being. His hands traced my waist as I turned, his face beautiful in the soft lights coming in from the city below us. Only the light could reach us here, not a single sound making its way into our solace. His eyes sparkled with it, worshipping every inch of me as I stood before him – in awe. As if my mere presence was a miracle put together by a random sequence of events.

A part of me wanted to ask if I reminded him of his wife, but I didn't want to mar the perfection of the moment. The look in his eyes was adoration mixed with pure, animal lust marked by the destructive rage of the monster within.

He quickly glanced at the necklace between my breasts, then up at my throat, a hint of recognition showing just briefly before he looked me in the eye again. His expression quickly reset, but I hadn't missed it.

"I, well, we…" he started, lush lips spreading into the most loving and wicked grin, "have a surprise for you."

His fingers traced lovingly down my arm, then he closed his hand around mine tightly.

"It's really a surprise for you both," he said, that grin never leaving his lovely mouth.

I felt my expression falter, but quickly fixed my lips into a considerate smile and squeezed his hand. His eyes shifted from brown to blue again – only for a second as Adam's presence within Emmett's body made itself known. I felt it like ants crawling over my skin, tiny legs working to cover my flesh entirely.

"Oh?" I asked. "Really?"

"Mmmmhmmm," Emmett hummed in response. "Adam thought it would be a promising idea to include the both of you in something instead of separating us. They won't be going away. We might as well work together in all ways, right?"

I thought for a moment, not once looking away from his eyes. He had a valid point, but the thought of his monster and mine carving their bloody path with us riding along and conscious of their actions made my heart lurch in my chest. My mind raced at the images flashing in my head. There had already been enough blood and carnage – and would continue to be as long as we lived, and our genes passed through time – but how much worse would it be?

How much more unchecked bloodshed would there be if we continued on this path? My heart almost ripped itself out of my chest at the thought, and I couldn't anymore. I had to see where this love took us.

Maybe I was enough to help Emmett keep Adam in check.

"I guess you're right," I said. "That never crossed my mind."

THE DARK OF YOU KINDRA SOWDER

"We were thinking about it after I told you about my wife. She wasn't like us. She was," he paused, frowning, "normal. She was our first of many. She was *food*. She has sustained us all this time until we could find another to make us whole again. Running through this world alone has been... difficult. More difficult than I could have imagined. Now that we've found you, we can't let go. Won't."

"I see," I said, looking down at the floor.

His hand came up to cup my chin, applying enough pressure so my head lifted, and our gazes met once more.

"I love you, Blythe. And Adam does too, in his own twisted way. How many other men will you find in your life that would love you and your monster? Would anyone else ever accept you?"

My mouth fell open in an attempt to reply, but my mind froze. No one else would because they didn't house this sinister presence like I did. There were dark people in this world – evil people. But they weren't anything like me. It took almost thirty years to find Emmett. How much more time could I really waste trying to find another that would accept both me and my monster because they also had their own?

THE DARK OF YOU Kindra Sowder

None. That was a simple answer.

The only thing to complicate all of this was the detective. I hadn't talked to Emmett about him at all, but how could I? That would put him in grave danger immediately for doing what came naturally to him. Protecting his own. Could I bring it up?

Not now. Maybe not ever. Another secret to take with me to the grave. Unless Cyra had mentioned him, but Emmett never once brought it up if she had.

He must have taken my silence as agreement because his eyes softened and he dropped his hand, taking my other one within it. He pulled me, guiding me toward the back room of his home. His version of my kill room, except his was much more elaborate – housing even a few medieval torture devices.

"Come with me," he said as he turned away from me, still holding onto one hand. "Hopefully, you'll like it. It took us some time to find the perfect one."

My heart hammered deep in my chest as Hyde reacted, growing stronger as we neared the darkest of places. We approached the double doors and then stopped. Adam lived so far in the open that it made me nervous. Then it made me wonder how many people had willingly walked through those doors expecting to have the best night of their lives only to end up as his victim, bleeding out as they watched Emmett's twisted face open wide to see the monster within.

Death darker than the largest void was housed behind those doors and even though I lived in such proximity to the same void myself, it stopped me in my tracks. My knees locked, and my feet began to ache in the six-inch heels I wore.

"Are you ready?" Emmett asked, startling me from my thoughts.

I jumped in my skin, my eyes ripping away from the double doors to rest on his face. Questions flooded me, taking residence in my expression. He noticed but didn't utter a word.

"Yes," I breathed with a slow nod. "I'm ready."

I wasn't, but how could I tell him that? Whatever stood behind those doors would be revealed soon, even if it weren't tonight. His earlier words led me to believe that.

Hyde bucked against my control as if she knew what lay beyond those doors. She pounded against

every part of me – every cell – making my head ache
with her impulses.

I barely paid attention as Emmett unlocked and
opened the doors, pushing them open wide to reveal
our prize for remaining. I gasped, revulsion nearly
causing nausea to rip a path up my throat. Hyde's
reaction was the exact opposite. She grew stronger at
the sight of so much blood and exposed flesh. I wanted
to run. We warred within the same body, but Hyde
would win this fight. The green gem resting against my
skin grew warm, glowing softly as if Hyde powered
something deep inside and it powered her in return.

I felt myself being pushed down into the dark
quickly. A man stood against the same St. Andrew's
Cross I had been tied to not long ago, his strong muscles
flexing as blood flowed from strategically placed gashes
– enough to bleed, but not bleed out. He'd bleed enough
for our monsters to take everything from him, and then
some. They'd take his life, then his heart. They'd take
his soul.

The soft recessed lighting illuminated the sweat
that trickled down his chest and forehead, his shoulder-
length hair sticking to his neck in drenched ringlets.
When he looked up at me and our eyes met, fear

replaced exhaustion, and his muscles rippled as he pulled against the restraints. It was as if he knew I wasn't there to save him.

Emmett let go of my hand and walked into the room, coming to stand next to the large man. Emmett was much larger, his Spartan lineage evident. The man began to scream, but Emmett/Adam reacted swiftly. Emmett's eyes turned blue as soon as the first note of terror hit the air, and he turned – punching the man in the jaw. Beads of sweat and blood flew, landing on the floor with finality. He fell silent quickly, not opening his mouth to scream again. Adam seemed proud as he looked at him. Like he was a prize, and he had fought hard for him. He looked at me and smiled. Adam was clearly in control now.

Hyde would follow close behind.

"We will share in death, my love," he said, a menacing smile spreading wide over his lovely face. "He will bleed until we are one. Forever."

THE DARK OF YOU KINDRA SOWDER

CHAPTER NINETEEN

Hyde pushed and fought against me even harder, clawing against my control. Every part of my body grew hot, my belly clenched with arousal, and the apex between my thighs throbbed with a desire that I was ashamed to admit to myself belonged to the both of us. I responded to Emmett's proximity. Hyde reacted to Adam and blood – the musk of terror that surrounded the restrained male. His sweat and blood mixed with it, creating a heady scent that swirled in my nostrils.

I closed my eyes and breathed in deep, mostly to steady myself. Hyde had other plans. She wanted what I fought against. I didn't want any more blood on my hands, but she thrived on it. Most of all, she wanted the heart that beat wildly in his chest. Somehow, I heard it beating rapidly in my ears alongside my own. I felt it beating in my chest and pulsing through my veins as if it belonged to me. As if this man before us lived within me as well.

Heat boiled up through my body and spread out from my core, taking residence in my eyes and brain. Every part of her flowed through me and pulsed with renewed life after I had pushed her down in the dark trenches for years. Yes, she had been active, but not in the way she felt she deserved.

Not in the way she *needed*. Not in the way she *craved*.

Opening my eyes, the renewed sight of the two men before me sent me into a tailspin. The room teetered, and the heat in my eyes grew until it seared. Then Hyde surfaced, and I was an unwilling passenger watching their descent into madness.

Tunnel vision swallowed me down until it looked like I was watching from the bottom of a deep, dark well. Nothing else mattered as Hyde pushed me down in search of depraved release.

Our shared body trembled as she sauntered almost seductively toward the two men, Adam smiling with the recognition of the one he genuinely loved. As Emmett said, he loved me in his own twisted way, but I wasn't Hyde. We were separate entities and always had been. Just like Emmett and Adam.

She came to stand before Adam, his eyes filled with obsession and adoration as his expression changed slowly with each passing second.

"Thank you," Hyde growled, placing her hand in the center of his chest.

His heart beat rapidly against our palm, warmth radiating off him that rivaled the sun.

"Anything for you," he said.

Our eyes shifted to the man beside us. He watched us with rapt fascination and horror, his brows furrowed, and wonderfully green orbs filled with confusion. The scent of him mixed with Adam's murderous intent wafted toward us again, causing the arousal we felt to increase exponentially. Almost to the point of pain.

Was this how they felt the night they took out their bloodthirsty hunger out on our shared bodies?

Hyde reached up, our perfectly manicured nails tracing the gash on the man's ribcage. It was deep enough to need stitches. That thought made Hyde purr audibly. The vocalization vibrated in our vocal cords, nearly turning into a deep monstrous growl. The man shrieked, the sound stopping abruptly once the realization moved into his expression that the screams would only make it worse. Little did he know his silence *wouldn't make it any better. He was brought there to die an elegantly agonizing death.*

There was no other purpose for him here.

Hyde looked up at him, meeting his terrified gaze. His eyes widened and he swallowed hard, seeing the demon that lay within. Knowing somehow that the woman who had been on the other side of the threshold was no longer in control and any dream of safety was an illusion.

She dug her fingers into his torn flesh, swirling her fingers within the ripped flesh and muscle slick with blood. The man's cries as she did this pierced our ears, our shared body rippling with pleasure as the torture continued for a few more seconds. She pulled our hand back, turning back to Adam. Bringing it to his lips, she rubbed the man's hot blood on his parted lips – breath coming in shallow pulls with the mixture of lust and death.

He leaned forward, taking our index finger into his mouth and sucking the blood from our flesh with a moan. His soft, warm tongue moved slowly around it to take in every bit of the man's essence. When the digit emerged again, it was licked clean. Our body hummed with thrill and excitement, arousal growing and growing until it was an almost painful point between my legs and the points of contact between skin.

The agony of it was exquisite.

And it still felt wrong.

Before Hyde could react, Adam's arm came around us and cupped our ass, pulling until our chests met. The need for him and what beat in the other man's heart only grew, enveloping us until that was all that existed. Our breaths mingled between us like twisted lovers. Adam's erection pushed against our abdomen – hard. Our shared vocal cords let out a thrilled, high-pitched gasp. She lifted our leg and wrapped it around his waist, Adam taking the hint. He lifted us until the aching spot between our legs met his arousal. Hyde ground into him, sighing as pleasure undulated through every nerve.

The groan that left him spurred her further. She ground against him again and nearly toppled over the edge. Adam's mouth descended on ours, kissing with such hunger it bordered on savagery. Hyde pulled back and gripped his strong shoulders, our nails digging in ever so slightly. A dark expression moved across his features, and I spotted Emmett's love within it. Despite what was happening, and what I knew would take place next, I focused on that. I allowed myself to revel in that love in an attempt to tune out the depravity that loomed.

"Not yet, my little butcher," Adam groaned. "We must attend to our guest first."

"Of course," Hyde said as she turned her attention back to the injured man, sliding down Adam's body until feet met the ground again. "We can't let it go to waste."

"No," the man said, shaking his head violently. "Please, no."

His entire body trembled with fear, adrenaline, and cold – goosebumps evident in the dim light. Hyde rode the high of the man's terror, the adrenaline flowing through our shared body driving her need to kill and her need to fuck like the animal she was. Bile rose into our throat, but she swallowed it down. It wasn't her reaction. It was mine. The mixture of emotions and the smells coming together would have caused me to vomit if I were in control. But I wasn't.

This was her show now.

"You know what happened to the last man who begged me for his life?" she asked the unnamed male, walking toward him until she stood nose to nose with him.

"W-wha-what?" he stammered.

Tears ran down his face, marking a path through the blood that marred his cheeks. Hyde acted on the impulse I felt coming. She leaned forward, opened her mouth, and licked the blood, sweat, and tears from his cheek. She did so slowly, moaning as our eyes rolled at the taste of iron and dread. She stopped at his ear, flicking our tongue back into our mouth and closing her eyes with distinct pleasure. She rolled the taste around in our mouth, ensuring it covered every inch to savor it further. When our eyes opened again, the man's eyes were wider than they had been before. I saw the urge to scream in his eyes, but he didn't. He just stared.

"I gutted him like the pig he was, ate his heart whole. For I am the big bad wolf the little piggies fear," Hyde replied, grinning. "And I plan on doing the same to you." She glanced at Adam who watched, absolutely fascinated. "But not before we have our fun."

I watched through Hyde's perception as the man's face fell even further, taking in the intent in our shared face – as well as Adam's. Emmett's monster was

205

just as bad, if not worse, than my own. They were one and the same. They were horror incarnate.

They were death, and it flowed out of their pores like smoke – coming out in a wall to blanket everything.

Hyde backed away, and Adam followed. He turned to face a long table at the far wall. Its surface glinted with tools of the trade along with some I had never seen before. They were old, a few covered in rust as if Adam hadn't bothered to care for them after using them.

"Pick your poison, my little butcher. You get every blow, and we'll deal his end together," he said, walking up to the table and grazing a long, silver ice pick lovingly with his index finger. His eyes sparkled with delight as they came up to meet mine again. "I want to see your depravity. I want to see your devotion."

I felt Hyde vibrating and jittering within our nerves, the smile spreading across our lips even more sinister than the last. She hummed with horrifying energy. So much I knew the man's torture wouldn't last long. When she inflicted this torture alone, she took her time. She wasn't as turned on by it like she was in

Adam's presence. She was the ravager of bodies. The mangler of souls.

She was so many things it was too difficult to name each part of her that I had seen over the years.

"With pleasure, my love," she purred seductively.

It didn't take long for her eyes to sweep over the artifacts on the massive table and settle on something. It never took her long to choose before meeting Adam either, but she didn't have the same array of devices to choose from in our kill room. And she stuck with some so crude they left mangled pieces behind. There was nothing clean about her kills, and there wouldn't be about this one either.

The device was a black collar made out of dark leather. In the middle was a two-pronged fork, the metal bar having forks on both ends. It was something new for both of us, but even I could admit I looked rather intriguing. And Hyde was drawn to it quickly. She reached out, touching it and taking the collar portion of it into her hands. The leather was smooth – brand new.

Her excitement grew as she touched it.

"The heretic's fork," Adam breathed from beside us, his warm breath on our neck. "Wonderful choice."

Adam toyed with the metal portion of the device between his fingers for a moment, admiring it with parted lips. His chest rose and fell quickly and forcefully as if he were breathing heavily. Our eyes scanned his form, the rigid erection obvious just like the tension of it in his shoulders. Hyde reached out and unbuttoned his suit jacket, then moved onto his button-down, removing both in one swift motion and dropping them to the floor between our feet. She took a step forward, chests almost touching, and reached out to trace his erection with her index finger as she licked her lips in anticipation.

"Do you want to do the honors?" he asked, holding up the collar as he sighed at the slight touch.

Dropping her hand, she licked her lips again, our shared arousal mounting as we noticed him watching the movement of our tongue across our crimson-painted lips.

"Absolutely," she replied.

She turned to the man she almost forgot existed in Adam's presence and grinned seditiously as she took the heretic's fork from his hands. Without ever seeing it before, the collar gave us both an idea of where it belonged. She closed the distance with only a few long strides and raised the collar so the man could easily see it in the dim light. His eyes widened and he shook his head like he was attempting to resist what he knew was coming for him.

He was at Adam and Hyde's mercy, and there was none to be had.

"No, please," he begged, tears falling down his sweat-stained cheeks. "No."

Without saying a word, she quickly fastened the collar around his neck and made certain the forked ends were in their rightful place. One rested against his broad chest just below the hollow where his collarbones met. The other prodded painfully against the soft flesh beneath his chin. The fork made the position awkward, but he couldn't look down to see what was being done without facing even more excruciating pain. The device wasn't deadly, that much I could tell, but his curiosity would be extremely painful.

Fresh beads of sweat rolled down the man's neck toward his chest. Hyde leaned forward, tongue outstretched and licked it away to taste his fear.

209

THE DARK OF YOU KINDRA SOWDER

As if on cue, I felt Adam's large hand grip one of my ankles and then disappear. The sound and feel of fabric being ripped away echoed in our ears followed by the sound of it landing some feet away. His hands came back and gripped our ankles again, pulling them apart so they were shoulder-width apart. Then his warm hands began to venture up and up until they reached the point of our shared arousal.

The hiss that left our mouth came from both of us as pleasure licked up our very core and ricocheted through every nerve. Hyde looked down, the urge to see his hand touching us above the silken fabric of the thong we wore as strong as her urge to maim. Teeth grazed bare flesh as Adam's other hand emerged from between our legs with a long silver-handled dagger. The sight of it nearly drove Hyde into a frenzy, but she controlled herself as he continued to move his fingers back and forth slowly.

Hyde gripped the blade, taking it from Adam and knowing its destiny. She raised it, tracing the tip of the blade along the lines of the man's abdominal muscles. He shrieked briefly until the tip of the heretic's fork pressed into the soft points of flesh below his chin, a single drop of blood emerging from within him. Hyde and Adam both moaned at the sight of it, Adam coming to stand at our back. He pressed firmly against the length of our body, completely bare flesh meeting ours. We felt the harsh tug of the thong being ripped from our body, laying us bare for him.

We looked back at him, and for the briefest moment, it was as if me and Emmett had a moment to ourselves. Adam's blues had given a small glimpse of Emmett's brown eyes, sharing the tiniest moment of love that could endure what was coming next.

As soon as Adam and Hyde took back control, she turned back to the man and sliced the dagger crudely against the man's flesh. He cried out through gritted teeth, refusing to open his mouth to endure the torture of the heretic's fork. Warm dark blood poured from him like a river down his stomach and legs. She sliced again. Once the man's cries echoed again, Adam's erection replaced his hand at our core. Even more pleasure rippled through us as his hands came up, gripped the heart-shaped neckline of the dress, and ripped it the rest of the way from our body. Every inch of skin was exposed as Hyde slashed at the man again, not striking the same place twice.

THE DARK OF YOU Kindra Sowder

Adam reached around and placed his palm against the man's quivering belly, coming away with the blood that would bind us forever. He wrapped his other arm around our waist, pulling us against him completely as his bloodied hand squeezed our breasts – smearing them with crimson as he moved against our slick heat.

The dagger dragged against the man's flesh again, penetrating the same spot she had first struck him. With a sputtering scream that could have shattered the earth, entrails poured out and onto the floor, bringing another barrage of the man's life with it. Hyde watched them fall and splatter on the ground sickeningly, quickly followed by the blood from the heretic's fork penetrating him beneath his chin and forcing its way inside his gaping mouth. She spied the sparkling silver within the dark cavern.

Somehow, the man was still alive through the onslaught, but he wouldn't be for long. The urge to end his life erupted between Hyde and Adam just like the pleasure that ran through them both. Adam's hand came to rest on top of ours, gripping the blade together.

"His death will bind us forever, my little butcher," he whispered into our ear with a groan.

THE DARK OF YOU   Kindra Sowder

They raised the blade together, and slowly dragged it across the man's throat, slitting his jugular.

As soon as the blade finished its work, Adam thrust deep inside us and cried out. The sound was animalistic – primal. Hyde dropped the blade to the floor. It clattered against the tiled finish and splashed in the growing pool of blood at our feet, each stroke coming with each new wave of life that flowed into the atmosphere.

The pleasure of it was earth-shattering and sickening all at the same time. If I could have closed myself off to it, I would have without hesitation. But I wasn't in control. Emmett and I had our moment within this chaos, and that was all we would be getting.

It wasn't long before both bodies climaxed as the dying man's last breath left his body, solidifying the bond only monsters could share.

That moment of life and death would bind our souls together for eternity.

As we tore open the man's chest and took his heart into our gullets, I spied the green statue across the room. The glow within her that ebbed and retreated beat in time with the gem at the base of my breastbone.

THE DARK OF YOU Kindra Sowder

Everything was linked and the bond between us would be nearly unstoppable.

CHAPTER TWENTY

The next evening, I sat in the middle of my living room floor as a fire crackled in the fireplace, a glass of deep red wine in my hand. It wasn't cold, but I felt chilled to the bone. Almost as if a sickness was settling in. There was, in a way.

Except it had always been there. It just didn't fight to hide anymore.

The events of the night before played over and over in my mind, and I dreamt about it in much the same fashion as I slept the day away. My entire body ached with the knowledge of what had taken place – of the life that was taken and the carnal outrage that came with it. The fact that it felt as good as it did and that I felt more at home than I had my entire life there in that room covered in Adam/Emmett's body and the other man's blood made me nauseous. It had never felt right before.

Bile rose into my throat as I watched the flames dance, throwing shadows across the walls. I swallowed it down with a large gulp of the wine. It burned the entire way down like I had been screaming. Maybe I had been in my sleep as the events repeated themselves. I still perceived the man's terror. I still felt the hopelessness that penetrated that fear. It skittered across my skin like ants, sending cold chills up and down my spine. Goosebumps spread over my flesh. The flames and the alcohol did nothing to warm me, and it probably never would again.

If this murderous instinct hadn't been cemented to my soul before, it surely was now. Hyde was more a part of me now than she ever had been, like what Adam said about the bond shared in the nameless man's blood chained us all together. It wasn't just his blood. We had also devoured his lifeless heart together, Adam still inside us – joined together in more ways than one.

"Sick like me," I muttered to myself, recalling the first message I had ever received from Adam Burnside with a dozen red roses. "Oh, my God," I nearly sobbed.

As soon as the sob left my throat, bile rose up again. Nearly dropping the glass to the floor, I jumped up and bolted to the kitchen. The sink was the nearest place to vomit and there was no way I could stop it.

THE DARK OF YOU   Kindra Sowder

It was bitter, sour, and bright red as I vomited up the wine I had been drinking all evening. It splattered on the sides of the stainless-steel sink, reminding me of the flow of blood after we had slashed the man's throat. The image of his intestines spilling to the floor at my feet, warm blood splashing my shoes and flesh, sent a fresh wave of vomit spewing from my gaping mouth.

Hyde remained silent as my stomach emptied completely.

"You have nothing to say, huh?" I coughed, spitting out the remnants that coated my mouth.

Nothing.

"Of course, you don't," I said to the silence. "You got what you wanted."

Technically, so had I. I wanted a relationship without her interference. With Emmett, I had that. Unfortunately, it came with a hefty price tag that I couldn't have predicted.

I hadn't heard from Emmett except for a text asking if I was all right. I answered it, letting him know I would be taking the day to rest, and I would see him later. I didn't rest. I dreamt of the tormented soul that died before my eyes, just like so many others before him. But his death served a deeper, higher purpose. That purpose had burned itself into every aspect of my being.

It was unbreakable, and unmistakable.

I stood and turned on the faucet, the water swirling down the drain to wash away my horror and shame. The sound of running water would have had a calming effect if it weren't for my racing thoughts and the humming electricity in my veins. It was interrupted by the distant vibrations of my cell phone, which I had intentionally left on the kitchen counter by the coffee pot after speaking to Emmett. I didn't make a move to answer it – just watched the water go down the drain as it vibrated against the countertop long enough for the person calling to realize I wouldn't be answering their call as the voicemail picked up.

Shutting off the water, deafening silence filled the apartment. The hum inside my body went quiet as well, not even the nausea or the internal noise of my own thoughts there to drown it out. I felt numb as I stood there, and I wasn't certain why. It was as if everything had fallen into a dark abyss that nothing could escape from.

THE DARK OF YOU   Kindra Sowder

Then the sound of my apartment door opening and closing shattered the silence, the sound of heels following and moving through the open air. My mind and body went on alert instantly, every muscle freezing in response to the sound. There were only two people it could have been, and I wasn't sure either of them were the ones that didn't mean any harm to me.

I didn't move. I didn't breathe.

"Blythe?" Lauren's voice floated to my ears.

I still wasn't certain I should answer. After our last conversation and the way she left the apartment without a word after seeing Hyde's kill room, there was no way she wouldn't have a cop at her back. I didn't hear another set of footsteps, but that didn't mean anything. Cops were trained to be sneaky and quiet-footed.

"You home?" she asked, making her way back from the bedrooms and toward the living room. "Blythe?"

There was pain in her voice as she approached the threshold into the living room, and that was how I knew she wasn't there to hurt me. At least, I hoped.

Feeling this deep down, I still hesitated. She had been my best friend for years – since before I started at the gallery. She had never steered me wrong, and I had never had reason not to trust her. Nonetheless, I hesitated. How *could* I be sure?

In this, I had to trust my gut. It had never pointed me in the wrong direction.

"I'm… I'm in here," I called out, my voice wavering with nervousness.

Within seconds, I turned to find Lauren standing in the doorway to the kitchen, her eyes wide and frantic. Her entire body was sheathed in black – leggings, a turtleneck, short skirt, and clunky boots that reached mid-calf. Her hair was thrown up in a messy ponytail, and not an ounce of makeup adorned her features.

"Thank God," she sighed, her shoulders visibly relaxing. "I tried to call you from the elevator."

"Yeah," I said, nodding toward the phone lying on the counter, "I heard."

"And you didn't answer?" she asked, a hurt look taking residence on her face.

"I wasn't sure if I should," I said with a shrug.

"Ummm, duh… you should," she nearly yelled. "I was worried. I tried to call you after I left too, and you didn't answer…"

"I was with Emmett," I interrupted.

"Oh," was all she said, taking a step forward.

"Right."

Silence enveloped us for a moment as we stood there watching each other. Finally, after the only sound the heartbeat in my ears, she took a deep breath.

"I wasn't sure if I should come over," she started. "I thought you may be mad at me."

"Well, you did kind of storm out without a word, Lauren," I answered. "To be honest, I wasn't sure if I should answer you when you called my name."

"Why?" she asked as if she didn't already know the answer. "I wouldn't have brought the cops, Blythe. It was just…" she paused, "a lot to take in. And seeing that room. It's been there all this time. You've been like this for all this time, and you didn't tell me. If anything, I think I had a right to be the one who was mad. You kept a big secret from me and I'm still your bestie, Blythe. Nothing, not even this... will ever change that."

I scoffed and tapped a finger on the countertop.

"It's not like I was keeping a secret affair from you, Lauren. I'm a monster. A killer. I tried to act like it was just Hyde, but it's not. After being with Emmett last night, I know that better than ever now. Excuse me if it wasn't something I could just come out and say to you while talking about work and guys."

"True," she said, her eyes flitting to the floor at her feet before she looked back up at me. "I should have said something before I left, Blythe. I'm sorry I didn't. I just wasn't sure what to say, or how. I needed a little time to sort my thoughts out."

"That's understandable," I said as I took a deep breath. "I've been there."

"I'm sure you have," Lauren said, a small glint of a smile surfacing. "How was it with Emmett last night?"

I let out a small laugh, knowing I couldn't tell her about what took place. She was already struggling with the knowledge she had. She wouldn't say it again, but I could see it in her eyes. She couldn't hide her emotions from me, and it made me feel horrible for hiding a whole other part of my life from her for so long.

"You don't want to know," I said matter-of-factly. "Trust me."

She nodded, watching me carefully. After another beat of silence, she smiled and cocked her head toward the living room.

"Girl's night in? Though it looks like you started without me," she joked.

"A girl's night in sounds great, actually," I answered.

"Yeah, it does," another voice came from behind Lauren along with the audible double-*click* of a handgun being racked.

I recognized the voice instantly and took a few steps toward Lauren's terrified face. How I hadn't noticed Cyra sneak in behind Lauren baffled me, but she was there with a small-caliber handgun pointed at the back of my best friend's head. Her bright pink hair peeked out from beneath a dark hoodie, her hand that held the gun steady. Her expression was resolute, a darkness in her eyes I had seen on more than one occasion since Adam made himself known.

In that instant, as I looked directly into Cyra's eyes, Hyde came biting back – ready to fight.

And it would be the fight of our lives.

BLYTHE and Hyde

will return soon

ABOUT THE AUTHOR

KINDRA SOWDER is from California but currently resides in South Carolina with her author/poet husband. Kindra has a MA in English Literature with a minor in Creative Writing specializing in fiction, and a BA in Criminal Neuropsychology. All of which she graduated at the top of her classes. Her greatest achievement is her son, Dechlin.

Keep up with Kindra on Facebook, Snapchat, Twitter, Instagram, TikTok, BlueSky, Lemon8, and her Amazon page.

All of her books are available in Audio, eBook, and Printed versions on Amazon, and wherever fine books are sold. If you do not see it, ask for it.

Also, by KINDRA SOWDER

THE EXECUTIONER TRILOGY (re-releasing soon)
Follow the Ashes
Follow the Screams
Follow the Bloodshed

THE PERMUTATION ARCHIVES
The Harvested
The Pursuit
The Scorned
The Defied
The Clash

THE INITIATIVE (re-releasing soon)

Chasing Shadows

THE MISS HYDE COLLECTION
A Bloody Heritage
Roots of Deceit
The Dark of You
Killer and the Sound (coming soon)

THE HEADHUNTER SERIES w/ Santiago Cirilo
Zombified
Resurrection
The Tribe (coming soon)

THE JOHN BAKER CHRONICLES w/ Bryan Tann
Invincible Heart
Unbreakable Mind

THE DARK OF YOU Kindra Sowder

VINDICTA w/ P. Mattern
An untitled second installment is being produced soon

ASHES OF HEAVEN (coming soon)

THE HOLLOW (a stand-alone multi-faceted horror
novel, coming soon)

PLEDGE (formerly on Vella, now being re-designed into
a full-length novel)

UNDER HELL'S WATCHFUL EYE

(Flash fiction)

THE DELIVERANCE OF DESIREE TANNER

(Flash Fiction)

AND MANY MORE . . .